RESCUED BY HER YETI

ALASKA YETI SERIES
BOOK 4

NEVA POST

ICICLE INK, LLC

Hello monster lover!

Thank you for joining Emma on her trip of a lifetime. Before we take off, please note that this book includes several close calls with a wildland fire, a neglectful ex-boyfriend, childhood abandonment (off page), and current fear of abandonment and disappointing others. Mature audiences will appreciate this sweet and steamy story about a human woman who's ready to take a walk on the wild side and the yeti she meets along the way who needs to learn to trust again. If this sounds right for you, enjoy! - Neva

For Mrs. Henderson.
Thank you for filling a book cart and dedicating the
first ten minutes of every English class to reading. I
looked forward to that break, which allowed a short
escape into a fantasy world. Hopefully, this book
provides the same escape for someone else (once
they're old enough). Please skip the spicy scenes if you
read this.

A firefighting yeti who sets her heart aflame.

Newly single and ready for adventure, Emma embarks on her dream canoe trip deep in the Alaska wilds. She doesn't expect to meet Yeshe, a real-life, firefighting yeti she nearly flashes in a meet-cute gone sideways. When a sudden fire traps her on his creek, Yeshe comes to the rescue, sweeping her into strong, furry arms. Their time together ignites a passion that burns hotter than wildfire. But one unforgettable week together isn't enough, and when their time is up, Emma wishes those furry arms will never let her go.

A rebel in disguise who challenges his rule against love.

Yeshe has always avoided romantic relationships, never imagining his world would collide with a city girl like Emma. But from the moment their paths cross, he finds himself drawn to her independence, determination, and hidden tattoos—just how many does she have? When a twist of fate brings her to his remote cabin and he saves her from a lightning-sparked fire, Yeshe can't resist a short-term fling. However, when lust turns to love, Yeshe reminds her their time is up.

A summer trip to Alaska and a rendezvous with a yeti is enough to convince Emma that North to the Future is a motto she can adopt, but can she convince Yeshe to let her in and take a chance on love?

CHAPTER ONE

Emma sat cross-legged on the living room floor of her Philadelphia apartment, surrounded by neat, organized piles of gear for her imminent solo canoe trip in Alaska. Months of planning were coming to fruition. A proud smile played at her lips even as a flutter of nerves danced in her belly. Finally, it was her turn to do something wild—in a well-thought-out and thoroughly planned way, of course.

Reaching toward the stack on her right, Emma plucked a small device from atop her PFD—personal floatation device. "Can you send me another test message, Agnes?"

Emma's long-time friend and neighbor kicked her feet up on Emma's coffee table. She took a pull from her iced coffee as she slid a finger across her phone's screen. "These messages come right to your satellite gadget?"

"Satellite communicator," Emma corrected.

"Right, that," Agnes said as she thumbed out a message.

"Yes. Or I can pair it with my phone to send and receive regular messages." Emma had discovered it was much easier to text from her phone than the communicator's small screen.

"You'll send me a text each day to check in while you're on your canoe trip?"

Emma nodded. "If you don't hear from me, please follow the emergency instructions in the document I emailed."

Agnes chuckled. "You mean your 'guidebook' entitled, *Birch Creek Emergency Support Plan?*"

"It's only a few pages."

"More than ten, with a table of contents and citations," Agnes replied as she side-eyed Emma.

No one could ever accuse Emma of being underprepared. She shrugged and turned on her communicator. "I'm going to be alone in the Alaska wilderness, and you're the only person who knows it. I'm taking enough chances as it is."

Agnes shook her cup, ice rattling as it settled.

"Under other circumstances, I'd advise against a secret, solo, canoe trip. But if anyone can pull it off, it's you, with all your planning and organization. You've seized every opportunity to get your boat on the water and dragged me to campgrounds to try out your tent." She paused, then added, "This entire trip . . . or, er, scenario, is something I'd expect from your sister, not you—the responsible twin."

Emma whipped her head up, her gut clenching. She disliked being compared to Gina, who'd shocked everyone by moving to Alaska last year, and whose past antics had prematurely aged their parents. "I'm nothing like my sister. I never organized midnight schemes to dismantle the rival high school's mascot. Never borrowed money from my parents or called them for help from a U.S. consulate in a foreign country. I went straight through college without causing any trouble and immediately landed a great job with benefits. I was the youngest person ever promoted to senior analyst in my company's history. My parents never have to worry about me."

An amused smile spread across Agnes's face. "Hmm . . . Gina dropped out of college to travel through Europe. When your parents wouldn't support her plan to go alone, she claimed to be traveling with a boyfriend—who she'd made up. You've told your parents and sister that you're going on a guided group canoe trip in Alaska with a boyfriend you are no longer dating . . . I'm seeing some similarities between your actions."

The knot in Emma's stomach cinched tight. She hated lying to her family and feared disappointing her parents. "But unlike Gina, when I initially told her and my parents about my plans, I wasn't lying. I *had* a long-term boyfriend, and I *believed* he and I were going on a guided group canoe trip."

But Derek, Emma's now ex-boyfriend, hadn't booked the trip like he'd promised. It'd conflicted with some trivial function at his country club. By the time she'd learned they didn't have a reservation, the trip had sold out. Emma's reasons for leaving Derek were too numerous to count, but this had been the one to push Emma over the edge. After years together, she'd kicked him out—made him move back into his penthouse—and planned her own canoe trip. A trip she'd come to realize that she desperately needed.

The promotions she'd earned and her new office at work were . . . well, not as awesome as she'd hoped. And that damn view from the coveted corner office window disappointingly included office workers like her in the building across the alley and dumpsters for the restaurant at the lobby level. With her latest career advancement came intimate familiarity of raucous garbage collection times. She had the title and the office but felt no closer to effecting real change in a stale company run by old men who'd seemingly never retire or be open to her ideas.

But out on the water in her canoe, all her disappointment melted away. She found peace, and the ability to focus on the moment and her surroundings in a way that didn't happen in the office. She'd finally allowed herself to take time for something that wasn't about building a safety net for her life. And Emma wanted to prove to herself that she could succeed outside of academia and a corporate office. For once she wanted to give in to her adventurous side.

Agnes's eyes narrowed. "I can't go with you because I have a trial, not to mention I can only paddle a canoe in circles. But why didn't you ask Gina to go with you? She lives in Alaska now and you're visiting her before and after your secret float trip."

A valid question, one Emma had considered. "She moved in with her ice climbing instructor and the family still knows virtually nothing about him. She hasn't even shared pictures of him. Regardless, she's 'new relationship' busy." That's what Emma kept telling herself anyway. Honestly, though, Emma wanted her own adventure. She'd lived in her sister's shadow for too long. If Gina went, Emma would feel like a tagalong on the expedition *she'd* planned. Emma didn't care that Agnes was the only other person to know about her trip. Once she'd canoed Birch Creek, Emma would know her capabilities surpassed achieving a solid grade point average and workplace synergy, she hoped.

She glanced at the satellite communicator and grinned at the message.

Agnes: You got this Em!

"Thanks," Emma said, turning off the device and placing it at the top of her neat stack. "I'm feeling good about my plans." At least, as good as could be expected, considering she'd lied to her family. "The charter plane company I'll be using to fly to Birch Creek received my folding canoe in the mail." It had cost a small fortune to ship, but it had to be done. An inflatable boat would have been fun on the creek and easier to transport, but she needed the canoe for the long crossing of Big Bear Lake at the end of her trip. Plus, Emma couldn't show up at her sister's house with a boat—the guided trip they thought she was taking provided boats. "And I've been through my checklist twice."

Agnes's straw hit the bottom of her drink with a loud slurp. "Let's not kid ourselves. You've been over your checklist more than twice."

Guilty. "Enough times to know that I have everything except bear spray. I'll need to buy that in Wildwood, when I'm at Gina's. Major airlines don't allow it in carry-on or checked luggage."

"Bear spray," Agnes repeated, blinking slowly. "You're choosing to go on a trip where you'll need pepper spray for bears. It's not too late to change your mind, you know."

Emma shook her head. She'd bought bear spray locally and practiced deploying it. Nothing—not even the possibility of furry, clawed beasts along the creek—would stop her from achieving her goal. She'd felt the same motivation to climb the corporate ladder. Hopefully, the result was better than the view from her office. "I'm determined. Plus, I'll get away from the ticks around here, so it's a tradeoff of sorts."

Agnes rolled her eyes good-naturedly as she stood. She offered Emma a hand up, then smothered her in a hug. "Text me when you get to Gina's tomorrow." She pulled away and added, "Send a picture of her boyfriend. I'm dying to know more about this Dorje fellow."

Emma was also eager to meet and learn more about Gina's boyfriend. She knew her sister . . . Gina was hiding something about Dorje, and Emma would figure it out soon enough. The irony. Emma would uncover her sister's secrets while hiding *her* true trip plans and a secret ex.

"I will," Emma promised as excitement eased her clenched gut. This time tomorrow, she'd be in Wildwood on the first leg of her Alaska adventure.

<hr>

YESHE CRAVED A PROPER SHOWER. After weeks spent fighting the Sweetwater Fire with the Aurora Crew, he daydreamed of steamy, hot jets of water to soothe aching muscles and rinse dark soot from his formerly-white fur.

He balanced a full plate of food in one hand as he swiped a fingertip across the picnic table in front of him. Grit coated his blue skin. "There's ash on everything in this campground." The Forest Service had closed the area to the public, which made it perfect for his yeti-friendly crew and catering contractor. Well, perfect except for the ash.

His friend, crew mate, and fellow yeti, Nima, slid his overloaded paper plate through the residue on the other side of the table. "There's ash all over *you*, from your furry head to your furry toes," he said, huffing a laugh. "Same as me. Has been since day-one on this fire."

Yeshe flashed his friend a wry smile as he hoisted his tired legs over the wooden picnic table bench and sat. "I know, I know. Hazard of being a wildland fire-fighter on mop-up. I'm just ready to not be dirty." He felt this way every summer, after every fire. He unrolled his shirt cuffs, tugging the yellow, fire-retardant fabric down to protect his no-longer-white fur from the ash when he leaned his forearms against the table.

Nima hummed in agreement around a mouthful of food. He swallowed and added, "Me too. You headed home tomorrow or to your brother's?"

Home was a log cabin on Little Caribou Creek accessible only by single-engine plane—bush Alaska was unique that way. "Dorje's," Yeshe answered before biting into his burger. Flavor exploded on his tongue as he enjoyed their first palatable food after weeks of MREs—meals ready to eat. He savored it for a moment before swallowing and adding, "I have some business in Wildwood." Yeshe usually needed alone time after spending weeks with their fire-fighting crew. But this time, he wanted to see his half-brother Dorje and Dorje's new girlfriend Gina.

Nima grinned. "So, you'll get your hot shower there."

"I could have a hot shower if I went straight home." Yeshe couldn't help the defensive note in his voice. "My outdoor setup is pretty damn good." He'd put a lot of work into the three-walled structure, piping water from a spring to a propane heater.

With a chuckle, Nima said, "The finest outdoor shower in Alaska." He paused, inspecting his burger. "Did you go with beef or veggie?"

Yeshe glance down at his plate. "They only had beef when I went through the line. You?"

"Veg," he said, looking thoughtful as he chewed. "It's pretty good." Poised to take another bite, he first asked, "What business do you have in Wildwood?"

Yeshe's stomach tightened with nerves. He didn't actually have any business *yet*. "I'm meeting with the folks at that Arctic Whimsy gift shop to discuss a consignment or wholesale deal for my carvings."

"It's about time," Nima said matter-of-factly. "You know the owners of the last house I worked on loved your custom cabinet knobs. Everyone raves about your work."

Yeshe did know—that feedback had given him the courage to set up this meeting, but he still had doubts. "You can't go wrong outfitting a second home along the Kenai River with hand-carved salmon handles on the kitchen cabinets." The owner had been an avid fisher. But would the yeti-friendly gift shop owners be as receptive?

As if reading his mind, Nima said, "The gift shop will love your work." His tone held more confidence than Yeshe felt. He added, "From what I understand, the homeowners at my next gig already ordered cabinet hardware. All chrome this time." When not fighting fires, Nima worked as a general contractor, picking up yeti-suitable carpentry and remodeling jobs around the state. But I'll keep putting in a good word for you whenever I can."

"Thanks, I appreciate it. Where's this next job?" Yeshe asked before polishing off his burger. There was one place everyone knew Nima *would not* be, and that was Wildwood. Nima hadn't set foot in the area since he'd broken up with Mari. His long-time girlfriend, now long-time ex, also grew up and lived in Wildwood. No one knew the details of their split, but Mari apparently got their hometown in the breakup.

"Denali. Should be a quick job. I'm not sure

what'll come after that." He eyed Yeshe's plate. "Where'd you get that cookie?"

Yeshe gestured to a pavilion across the campground. "End of the table by the grill."

While Nima searched for dessert, Yeshe pulled out his phone to message Dorje about his plans to visit. Thankfully, the campground had cell coverage. At home, he needed to pair his cell phone to a satellite communicator to send a text. Not that he sent many. Yeshe's world, and social circle, was small. He opened his messaging app and tapped out a note to Dorje and Gina.

> Yeshe: I'll be rolling into Wildwood tomorrow night around 9. Can the crew drop me at your place?

Gina responded almost immediately.

> Gina: *red heart* Yay! Can't wait to see you!!

She'd been so good for Dorje, and her enthusiasm for everything in life made Yeshe smile. She quickly sent a second message.

> Gina: You'll get to meet Emma, my sister!!!

Yeshe's smile faded with that news. There'd be another person at Dorje's house? Four would be a crowd. He waited for a pool of dread to settle in his middle or for his mind to conjure an excuse to go straight to his cabin instead of Wildwood, but neither happened. He liked Gina. Maybe he'd like her twin, too, though Gina had insisted she and Emma were nothing alike.

> Dorje: Let yourself in. G and I will
> be out tomorrow night.

Yeshe paused. With he and Emma both there, all the bedrooms would be taken.

> Yeshe: Which bedroom will I be in?

> Dorje: Uh, yours?

> Gina: Your bedroom . . . Same as
> always. Emma will be in the
> guestroom.

Yeshe *had* been using the same bedroom since he was a teen, but he still had trouble trusting it was *his* room. Yeshe's parents, both yeti, had been lousy role models. Thanks to the absentee father he and Dorje shared, Yeshe had learned he could only count on himself. And some lessons were hard to unlearn, especially when they'd served Yeshe fine so far.

"No more cookies," Nima announced as he sat back down at the table. "But they have cake. Brought you a piece."

Yeshe looked up from his phone as Nima slid a small plate toward him through the ash. "Thanks," he added absentmindedly.

Nima speared his cake with a fork. "What's wrong?"

Yeshe blinked. He no more wanted to talk about how his lonely childhood had made him distrustful of adult relationships than Nima wanted to discuss his breakup with Mari. "Gina's sister Emma will be in Wildwood, staying with her and Dorje."

White eyebrows rose in response. "Does she know about yeti?"

"I wondered the same. But she'll have met Dorje before I arrive." Yeshe quickly tapped out another message.

> Yeshe: Does Emma know I'm a
> yeti?

He didn't want to let himself into Dorje and Gina's house only to startle their guest, who'd be home alone. Most humans weren't aware yeti existed. Dorje had taught Gina several ice climbing lessons before she'd accidentally discovered the truth. Dorje's neck gaiter, worn under his ski goggles to cover his entire face, had slipped, revealing himself, and the entire yeti race, to her. Luckily, Gina loved what she saw. But not all humans were as accepting. And many wouldn't hesitate to make a quick buck by taking and selling a picture, exposing yeti to unknowing humans and threatening their lives. Yeshe shuddered at the thought.

> Gina: This time tomorrow, Emma
> will know about yeti, including you!
> But she'll probably be jet-lagged
> and in bed early. So you'll meet her
> the next morning. Can't wait to see
> you! *heart eyes*

Her choice of emojis made him smile. In the few months since Gina had entered Dorje's life, she'd become like a half-sister to Yeshe, doubling his family of one. He wasn't entirely sure what to make of it. But as he reread the text string, warmth spread through him. It reminded him of when Dorje's human grandmother, Nana, had been alive and done everything she could to make Yeshe feel welcome.

"Gina's assuring me Emma will know about us," Yeshe relayed to Nima.

"Well, then. Guess you'll make a new acquaintance," Nima observed. Yeti didn't meet new people often. How could they when their kind were hidden from most of the world?

"Guess I will," Yeshe agreed, surprised at his casual acceptance of the news. He tapped out a quick response.

> Yeshe: Looking forward to seeing you both too.

Even the new person, Gina's sister Emma.

CHAPTER TWO

Yeshe's jaw cracked with a wide yawn as he hoisted his bag over his shoulder and waved a casual thank you to the crew rig. If the weather stayed hot and dry, he'd see them again soon enough. Gravel crunched under the truck's tires as it pulled out of his brother's driveway.

Before letting himself into Dorje's house, Yeshe stepped onto the deck to enjoy the impressive summer evening view of Fireweed Valley below. Sharp mountain ridges glowed in the low-angle sun, casting shadows on the white and turquoise ribbons of Fireweed Glacier and the rocky outwash plain splashed with green vegetation. Smoke from the distant Sweetwater Fire dulled the view with a distinct reddish-orange haze.

Yeshe yawned again as he checked the time on his phone. Nine-thirty. Dorje's truck wasn't in the driveway, so he and Gina were still out. Probably a good sign. Emma would have met Dorje today and learned about yeti. If she'd freaked, they wouldn't have kept their evening plans . . . He hoped. He didn't want to startle her.

Once inside, Yeshe moved quietly through the house and down to first floor. Its small open area had an old couch and bookshelves lining a wall, still holding Nana's beloved paperbacks. Three doors on the other wall led to Yeshe's room, a bathroom, and the spare room where Emma should be sleeping.

He wearily dumped his bag in his room, careful not to make too much noise. He needed sleep, hours and hours of sleep. But first, he'd take that shower he'd been longing for.

Yeshe yanked his shirttail from his pants, undoing its buttons before retrieving his toiletry bag and heading to the bathroom. They could have divided the spacious room into a snug private bath for each of the downstairs bedrooms. But Yeshe liked it as it was, plenty of room for a seven-foot-tall yeti.

The bathroom had a large window, currently covered with a shade. Huh. He'd never noticed the shade before tonight. It wasn't like anyone would walk by and look in. Dorje didn't have close neighbors. Plus, the deck above shielded the downstairs windows, which offered views nearly as stunning as those from upstairs. The shade wasn't needed.

Shrugging it off, Yeshe pulled his toothbrush from his toiletry bag, striped it with toothpaste, then ran it under the sink before moving to stand in front of the window. He tugged open the shade, brushing his teeth while admiring the view.

A muffled sound from the other bedroom caught his attention. He turned as he heard Emma's door open and hurried, bare footfalls along the hall's wood flooring. He hadn't yet closed the bathroom door or turned on the light since he'd opened the shade.

Emma stepped through the open doorway, mumbling under her breath in a way that signaled distracted confusion. A purple eye mask covered her forehead, its strap tangled in her auburn hair. She wore snug short-shorts that hugged her backside and a tank top that barely contained the loveliest breasts Yeshe had ever seen. Though, to be fair, he hadn't seen many.

She curled her fists around the hem of her tiny, lavender-colored top, sliding it up creamy skin and exposing a small bird tattoo. He jolted to his senses as he caught sight of the enticing bottom curve of her breast.

"Whoa, whoa, whoa!" He sputtered around his toothbrush, rushing to alert her to his presence before she pulled her top all the way off.

Emma jumped a mile and shrieked.

So much for not disturbing Dorje and Gina's jet-lagged guest.

***

"WHAT ARE you doing in my bathroom?" Emma stammered, her heart practically leaping out of her chest. A giant *yeti* had just scared the shit out of her.

Yeti. Meeting Gina's boyfriend hadn't been a dream. Her twin had secrets alright. She was dating a friggin' yeti. And here was his brother.

The yeti held up a big, cobalt finger in a universal "one sec" gesture as he spit toothpaste into the sink and rinsed his mouth. "Little bird," he said, his deep voice rumbling in a nipple-hardening kind of way, "this is the *guest* bathroom. While we're both visiting Dorje and Gina, we're sharing it. This is *our* bathroom."

"I'm aware," Emma managed sheepishly. "You startled me. I wasn't thinking clearly." Had he called her "little bird" because he'd seen the swallow tattoo? She crossed her arms over her chest, covering her now-pebbled nipples and the tattoo, once again concealed under her too-thin tank top.

"What did you call me?" she asked into the awkward silence.

"Little bird." His sapphire-blue gaze cut unerringly to her concealed ink. "You have a swallow tattoo on your side, under your arm."

So many people displayed their gorgeous head-to-toe body art, but Emma's ink had been a private act of rebellion. If her swallow had been visible, Derek would have seen it right away. Instead, she'd gotten it, and several other tattoos, in places on her body where a boyfriend should have noticed. Only he never had. One more reason she'd made Derek an ex.

Emma took a moment to calm her racing heart and whirling mind. She'd only been in Alaska a few hours and might have flashed her boobs at a *yeti*, who'd *immediately* noticed her body art. "Please don't say anything to Gina, I haven't had a chance to tell her yet." She'd tell her sister about her tattoos eventually but didn't want to explain them until she also told her family about her breakup with Derek.

Quirking his sky-blue lips, he drew an X over his

chest. His *naked* chest. His plaid shirt hung completely open, exposing defined pecs and abs—despite fur covering them—that disappeared under the waistband of his pants. Emma did her best not to bite her lower lip. Yeti were her sister's thing, but . . . Wow.

"I won't tell," he said as he offered her his hand. "I'm Yeshe, by the way. Dorje's brother."

"Emma," she replied, regarding him in a serious, business-like manner—the mode she was most comfortable with—as if they were greeting each other over a conference room table. At least until her palm pressed against his, and her focus shifted to his huge, cornflower-blue hand gripping hers. His skin was equal parts rough, like a construction worker's might be, and smooth, like an old leather-bound book.

"I'm Gina's sister, but I think you know that." She refocused on his face. Yeshe's white beard—or was that fur?—was longer than Dorje's. Not unkempt, just a little . . . wild. Weathered cerulean cheeks suggested he'd spent a lot of time outdoors.

"Your eyes are a different color than your brother's," she mumbled as she lost herself in clear, deep pools of blue. She'd never seen anything like them and they left her momentarily mesmerized.

"Excuse me?" He slipped his hand from hers.

Heat flushed Emma's cheeks as embarrassment flooded her. Why had she been studying his eyes so intently, and why had she commented on them? Could she be any more awkward? *Shake it off, Em.*

Emma backed up, crossing her arms over her chest again. "I was simply making an observation. I'd never seen a yeti before meeting Dorje—and now you. Your eyes are . . ." She swallowed down her embarrassment. "Striking." That was fine to say. It was true. Why deny it?

Yeshe grinned, and his eyes shone even brighter. "And I *observe* that your hair is darker than your sister's."

Her hand darted to the wavy strands—they probably resembled a raven's nest after her restless night of sleep, if her current grogginess and befuddlement were any indication. "It's brown."

Yeshe cocked his head and moved closer, ghosting his fingertips over her unruly waves. "I'd call it mahogany."

Emma froze at his almost touch, holding her breath. She liked the intensity of his attention. No one had ever studied her like this.

"You have beautiful streaks of red mixed with a rich red-brown. Reminds me of a piece of wood I once worked."

That wasn't a comparison she'd ever received, but she oddly liked it—coming from him. "Thank you, I think. My sister said you were in town to sell your wood carvings."

Yeshe stepped back and buried his hands in his pants pockets. "Yeah, I'm hoping to make a sales agreement."

"Good luck," Emma managed around a yawn while she pulled a towel from the rack. "Listen, I totally overslept. Gina might have mentioned I'm in Alaska to go on a river trip? I'm surprised she didn't wake me up." She paused briefly and lowered her voice. "But it's really quiet upstairs. She and Dorje must still be asleep."

Yeshe's lips twitched, and his focus again slid to her hair . . . No, to her eye mask. "Your sister and Dorje are still out. It's nearly ten o'clock—at night." He gestured toward the window. "Welcome to the Land of the Midnight Sun."

His words took a moment to sink in, but when they did, Emma spun to look out the window, then snatched up her phone. She glanced at the time on the phone's screen, to the light outside, then back to Yeshe, who appeared to be biting his lip so he wouldn't laugh. She'd spent months preparing for this trip, knew the summer sun didn't even set in parts of Alaska—she'd gotten a tattoo to commemorate it for goodness' sake—and already the daylight had fooled her. "Right. Well, I've never been this far north. This is new to me."

He offered a sympathetic smile. "I hear that happens to a lot of visitors."

Emma fought a swallow. "So, I slept for an hour, barged in on you thinking it was morning, and nearly took my shirt off in my rush to hop in the shower."

Yeshe shrugged. "That sums it up. A memorable meeting."

Emma squeezed her eyes shut and grimaced. "Let's start over in the morning," she said as she hastily rehung the towel and backed toward the door. "I'm going to bed. Again." Before Yeshe could notice her head-to-toe blush, she scurried down the hall.

"Sleep well, little bird," he said, his deep voice floating after her before the bathroom door clicked shut.

Little bird. She took a ragged breath as she tried to slow her pulse. *I am not attracted to the yeti with the sapphire eyes.* No, that was another of her sister's things, and Emma's preferences were usually opposite Gina's. But she couldn't deny Yeshe's baritone voice and sweet nickname for her made the hairs lift on her arms—in a good way.

But it didn't matter. Emma had traveled to Alaska to fulfill a personal goal, not ogle the locals. She couldn't afford distractions. While she excelled at many things, lying challenged her. And yet, she had many a lie to tell. Fearing her parent's disapproval and her sister's intervention, she'd fibbed about her solo plans. And now that she'd met Gina's boyfriend, and his brother, she couldn't tell Agnes the truth or share photos—Emma would keep the yeti secret.

Once Emma cast off from the banks of Birch Creek in two days, it would all be worth it, she was sure.

CHAPTER THREE

Emma lifted a corner of her eye mask. Bright light glowed around the guestroom window shade's edges. Was it finally morning? Or was it still the middle of the night, only hours since she'd encountered the blue-eyed *yeti* in the bathroom? She stifled an embarrassed groan as she reached for her phone. Had she really almost pulled her top off in front of him? How much had he seen? Not that she could do anything about it now.

She confirmed the time on her phone—seven-thirty *in the morning*—then slipped out of bed, opened her door a crack, and peered into the hallway. Yeshe's door remained closed. She ducked into the bathroom, managing to shower without flashing anyone. First hurdle cleared, no awkward repeat of last night.

With a warm summer breeze coming in the window, Emma tugged on shorts and a T-shirt. She kept her hair down to hide a tattoo on the back of her neck and covered another on her ankle with her socks. Because of the conservative dress code policy at work that didn't allow bare legs or sandals, no one there had seen it. Plus, people saw—or didn't see— what they expected. And none of her friends or coworkers expected Emma to sport an astrological sign on her neck.

As she climbed the basement stairs, noise from the kitchen floated her way. She paused when Dorje came into view. The giant yeti filled a teakettle, then rinsed a container of strawberries before removing the tops and slicing them on a cutting board. The big guy's task prepping the small, delicate fruit endeared him to Emma.

Leave it to Gina to not only discover *yeti* after moving to Alaska, but to date one of the mythical creatures. Her sister *always* had to push the boundaries and be unique. Well, she'd succeeded this time.

As Emma crested the stairs, Gina came out of her and Dorje's bedroom. "Good morning," she cried, enveloping Emma in a tight hug. "I still can't believe you're in Alaska. Did you sleep well? The four-hour time change from the East Coast is a killer. Did your eyes pop open at like three this morning?"

"I woke up early in the night," Emma admitted, not sharing that she'd nearly stripped in front of Dorje's brother. "The midnight sun takes a little getting used to."

The stairs creaked as Yeshe ascended. Today he wore a sporty, short-sleeved, snap-up shirt and board shorts, an outfit that showed off furry arms and legs. A pair of sunglasses rested on top of his head. Confidence rolled off him even as he looked ready to relax on the deck. He was clearly comfortable in his own skin. She found it undeniably attractive, and her middle fluttered. *Damn it!*

"Yeshe!" Gina cried, crossing the room to wrap him in a hug like the one she'd given Emma. "It's so good to see you. Come meet my sister."

Yeshe wrapped an arm around Gina in what looked like brotherly affection. Gina appeared to have found some genuinely good people—er, monsters?

Gina turned to her. "Emma, this is Dorje's brother, Yeshe."

Emma's shoulders tensed, reluctant to admit

she'd barged in on their other guest in the bathroom last night.

But Yeshe simply extended a hand, a small smile on his cerulean lips and a twinkle in his eye. "It's nice to meet you at last, Emma," he said, like they'd never met before, as if she hadn't nearly flashed him last night. "Gina mentioned that you're in Alaska for a river trip."

Right. Okay. Last night's encounter was their secret. Excellent. The yeti had good judgment. They really were starting over this morning. Emma returned the greeting. "Nice to meet you as well. And yes, I'll be taking a trip of a lifetime." Truth. She just hadn't shared her *actual* trip plans.

Dorje looked up from his cutting board. "We're glad you could visit. Sorry that your boyfriend . . ." He waved his knife as though struggling to recall his name.

"Derek," Gina supplied. She raised an eyebrow and added, "The billionaire bad boy." Gina had never liked Derek—a feeling that had been mutual.

"He's not a billionaire," Emma corrected. Only a millionaire, and none of it earned. Maybe if he'd had to work for it, he'd be a more conscientious person.

"Right, Derek," Dorje continued. "He'll arrive in

time for your charter flight from Anchorage tomorrow?"

Emma nervously clasped her hands behind her back to keep from winding a strand of hair around her finger—a tell that she was lying. She'd learned to occupy her hands at work when she told white lies, not that it happened frequently. *Excellent report, sir. Couldn't have written it better myself.*

"That's the plan," Emma confirmed. Well, that had been the original plan.

Yeshe offered Emma a mug of coffee, then asked, "Which outfitter are you using?"

A wriggle of nerves played in Emma's stomach, and she placed both hands firmly on her mug. She'd expected this question and rehearsed answering it. Though it made her slightly ill, she needed to give them brief details based on her original itinerary with Derek. A sickening thought hit her as she said, "Wild Alaska Outfitters." Dorje worked for Mountain High Guiding Service. Did he know the guides with WAO? Would they quickly learn she was lying? Her mouth dried, as if her body was making it more difficult for her to speak another untruth. To combat it she sipped at her coffee. It had to be done if she wanted her canoe trip.

"On the Arctic River?" Yeshe asked, and Emma

gave a quick nod. It was the most popular trip and the one she thought she'd be on.

"WAO is well-respected. And fishing on the Arctic is excellent," he said as Gina ushered everyone to a table on the sunny deck with a stunning view of Fireweed Glacier. The smoke had cleared overnight, unveiling a breathtaking panorama of jagged mountain ridges and white-blue glacier.

The coffee had not only moistened Emma's mouth, but the caffeine provided a little boost of courage. "I've read that," she replied brightly, because she *had* read it. Her answer was honest, even if it made it sound like she couldn't wait to catch her own dinner. But in truth, she wouldn't know *how* to catch her own dinner, and she'd be paddling Birch Creek instead. An, ahem, rather large, secret detail.

Sliding into a chair across from Emma, Gina asked, "Did you say that you and Derek took canoe lessons?"

They'd both begun the lessons, but only Emma had finished them. "Yeah, we started in a pool this winter, then I transitioned outdoors in spring. There's an active canoe group in Philly." Her new canoeing friends were a vast improvement over Derek's shallow acquaintances. "It's been great."

Besides canoe practice, weightlifting had been a vital part of Emma's trip planning, and she was proud of the muscle definition in her arms. She thought back to nearly lifting her shirt over her head in front of Yeshe. Would he have noticed how her biceps popped when she did that? *God, I hope so . . . Wait, no! What's wrong with me? Stop thinking about Yeshe that way! Focus on your float trip!*

Yeshe added, "Water travel is pure bliss when conditions are good, but it's unforgiving under the wrong circumstances. It's smart to take lessons, spend time on the water, and prepare. Like you did with ice climbing, Gina."

Her sister plucked a strawberry from her plate and glanced at Dorje. "Nothing wrong with learning a new skill."

"I totally agree," he said. "Are you familiar with the ten safety rules, Emma?"

"They're taped to my water bottle," she admitted. She'd memorized them.

The big yeti nodded his approval and raised his coffee mug to Emma's in a salute. "Excellent, I'm glad to hear it."

She couldn't help but grin like she'd received a gold star. "There is one item I still need for the trip—bear spray." Emma turned to Gina. "Do you have time today to drive me to the sporting goods store? Wildwood Cycles carries it, if my research is correct."

Gina's face pinched. "I have tutoring clients this morning, and my car is in the shop." She turned to her giant boyfriend. "But you could use Dorje's truck. He won't need it. He'll be assembling the new grill today. We've invited friends over for a potluck while you and Yeshe are here."

Dorje nodded in agreement. "It's all yours. Can you drive a stick?"

"Derek taught her," Gina said, eyes sparkling. "He has a Porsche. A red Porsche," she amended, "with a manual transmission."

Fuck. Emma's stomach clenched. It was only natural that Gina would bring up Derek, but she really wanted to put him behind her and stop telling lies. "Not yet," she said, forcing out another false-hood. The truth was, Derek wouldn't let her drive his car. She'd asked. He'd refused. It made her hot under the collar to think about.

Yeshe helped himself to a second slice of quiche and offered, "I also need to run an errand. I can drive you into town in Dorje's truck."

Emma hated lacking the skill to do something relatively common and that she'd dated someone who'd refused to teach her. And now she felt like a burden. Yeshe probably had his own plans. She did her best to swallow those feelings and flashed what she hoped was a grateful smile. "Thanks, I'd appreciate that," she said, before realizing she'd just agreed to go into town with a yeti. Gina had said most humans didn't know about yeti, and the yeti wanted to keep it that way. So how exactly was this going to work?

YESHE GLANCED OVER AT EMMA, his silent companion, as they bumped down Dorje's narrow driveway. She curled and released tanned fingers around the door handle several times while her knee bounced. Was she nervous to be in the truck with him? Or annoyed that he'd acted like they hadn't met last night? When Gina had introduced them this morning, he'd found he'd wanted to keep last night between himself and Emma.

"Everything okay over there?" he asked, glancing in her direction.

She released the handle and turned to him. "I'm sorry you have to take me into town. I don't want to be an inconvenience or put you in danger of being seen by, well, anyone."

He eased his own grip on the steering wheel as relief loosened his tense muscles. Was that all? "It's no bother. I'd planned to visit the Arctic Whimsy gift shop this morning to discuss sales of my wood carvings. Wildwood Cycles is down the street." He paused, then chuckled. "Consider this carpooling."

"Okay . . . But why are you laughing?"

"Because I've never actually carpooled before. I don't own a vehicle—there aren't any roads where I live. I'll hop on a small plane to get home." When the corner of Emma's mouth lifted, his smile widened. He liked that he'd made her grin.

"I can't even imagine that," she said. "I'm glad I can give you the excuse to try something new. But seriously, thanks. I hate to be a burden."

Burden? Despite being reclusive, he felt lucky to have the chance to spend time with Emma today . . . He wasn't sure why. Usually, he minimized *all* relationships, even the non-romantic kind.

"You're not a burden," he assured her.

Emma sighed and gave him a look like she didn't really believe him before gesturing to the gate at the end of the driveway. "I'm guessing this keeps people out and protects the yeti secret."

"That's right. The fewer that know, the better. Bigfoot hunters are everywhere. Occasionally the wrong person sees us, blurry photos hit the media. Biologists usually claim it's a rare albino moose or a *white,* brown bear. Despite living off the grid, I've read enough books and seen enough movies to know what happens when the government finds a new intelligent species."

Emma stared at him. "Then how is this trip to town going to work? I'm nervous for you." She gestured toward the sun. "The truck has tinted windows, but people can still see in. This seems like a tremendous risk. What if you get pulled over by the police? What if someone sees you and takes pictures?"

Yeshe opened his mouth to respond, then closed it again. He'd never met someone so concerned about his welfare. Well, aside from Dorje and Nana. He liked that Emma cared, but he wasn't used to being fussed over like this.

"A calculated risk." He gestured to his body. "I put on jeans, a white hoody, a ball cap, and sunglasses. Despite my size, I know how to blend in when I need to. Life is full of risks, and I'm willing to take this one. I won't let fear of what-ifs keep me from what I want." Yeshe tolerated risk alright, as long as it didn't involve his heart.

She glanced at him, then back to the road. "You're right. Life revolves around taking and minimizing risks. I get it."

"I appreciate your concern, though," he said as he maneuvered a series of potholes in the narrow alley behind the gift shop. "I'm parking behind the building I'm visiting. It's only a few steps from the truck to their backdoor. I'll stick to the back rooms which don't have customers. The owners know about yeti and how important it is to remain discreet." He pulled into a vacant spot where a tall white fence with peeling paint shielded the driver's side. "See," he said, "We're sheltered here."

Emma craned her neck. She glanced around before gazing up at the building's eaves. His lips quirked. She was cute. "Any surveillance cameras up there? Is the coast clear?" he asked.

He joked, but Emma gave him a serious, no-nonsense jerk of her head. "All clear," she confirmed before climbing down from the truck. As he stepped out, she circled the vehicle before stopping to give him an appraising look. Small, efficient hands tugged at his hood, covering more of his face around his ball cap.

Yeshe gestured to the building's backdoor. "I'm not going far," he said, "I'll be—"

Loud laughter cut him off, and in one super-human tug Emma brought his face down to hers, her back against the fence. "Slip those giant arms around me," she hissed. "Hide your cobalt hands between my back and the fence, or those people will see them."

Yeshe could have shoved them into the pocket of his hoody, but he didn't. Not with Emma's arms around him, her cheek nearly brushing his, her intoxicating sweet summer clover scent enveloping him.

He wrapped his arms around her, sliding his hands up her back. Emma's firm, warm body felt like it was meant to be tucked against his. He closed his eyes and inhaled deeply as he allowed himself to sink into the embrace—they had to look convincing, after all.

She thinks my eyes are striking.

Yeshe quickly chased away that line of thought. Emma had a boyfriend . . . granted, one who'd never taught her how to handle his stick. He inwardly snickered at the double entendre. Yeshe could do better than Not-A-Billionaire Derek in *so* many ways. He murmured, "I can teach you how to drive a stick." Her face was so close that his lips brushed her ear, and she gasped as if startled.

Yeshe tried to pull back but met resistance. Emma had cinched her arms tightly around him, the mounds of her breasts teasing his chest. Gods, he loved it. Was that wrong? This woman could never be his. She lived in a city and had a boyfriend. Yeshe lived alone—by choice—in the wilderness.

"Have those people moved on?" he asked, his voice hushed. Emma had a better view of the alley.

She stiffened. "What? Oh, yes, um, all clear now." She quickly dropped her arms and sidled away, fanning her face as if the sun's heat was too much for her. "Don't worry, you don't need to teach me how to drive a manual."

He crossed his arms. "What if I want to?" If she could have driven herself today, she wouldn't have felt like a burden on Yeshe. He'd help her avoid a situation like this in the future if he taught her to drive. Emma regarded him, her greenish-gray eyes reminding him of shiny fish scales—beautiful to him. He kept his compliment to himself. He'd already compared her hair to a chunk of wood, and no woman appreciated being likened to a trout or spawning salmon fresh from the sea.

"You really don't mind?" Her tone dripped with

skepticism, as if a driving lesson would hugely inconvenience him.

"We have a few hours until the potluck. I'll take you to a private airstrip. Few planes use it, mostly our friend Dale. It's where Nana taught me and Dorje to drive. We can text our change of plans to him and your sister."

A slow, beautiful smile lit Emma's face, and her eyes turned a deeper shade of green, more like a mossy creek rock. *Stop noticing that shit, Yesh. Emma is not for you.*

"I'd love that, Yeshe. Thank you."

"No problem." It truly wasn't. He looked forward to teaching her. "Meet me back here when you're done? I'll be at the truck."

"I'll hurry, so you're not waiting for me," she said before turning on her heel.

"Don't rush on my behalf," he called. Then, after too long of a pause, Yeshe tore his eyes away from the curve of her ass and turned toward the gift shop.

He took a deep breath, adjusted his hat, and prepared to negotiate his first business deal. Time to live up to his word, take this risk, and not let fear of rejection stop him now.

CHAPTER FOUR

Emma quickly covered the two blocks to Wildwood Cycles. It looked like the store specialized in bikes but sold running and hiking shoes in addition to kayaks. A small-town store fitting the needs and interests of the locals.

A prominent display of bear spray canisters greeted every customer who walked in the door. Emma grabbed two canisters, then turned down an aisle lined with guidebooks. She paused in front of a collection of paddling books, not actually focusing on what was in front of her, but replaying the scene in the alley next to Dorje's truck. Had she really plastered herself against a yeti? Yes, yes she had.

She'd been trying to protect Yeshe, hide his blue hands and face, by . . . uh . . . pressing her body against his as if they'd been in a lovers' embrace. It'd been a snap decision. But he'd felt so good against her, so big and strong. He was solid muscle. His fur, soft on the ends and coarse closer to his skin had rubbed her cheek, sending goosebumps down her arms, while his aromatic, smoldering log scent made her eyelids flutter shut.

It reminded her of camping trips during her youth. Of carefree happiness, when she and Gina had *both* been daring—the two of them eager to explore and experience everything. Before Emma cared how those choices might affect her parents and others. Gina had remained carefree, while Emma had reined it in. But Yeshe's scent had triggered something in Emma, the part of her that had planned a solo canoe trip. It both thrilled and scared her. She needed to tread with caution.

Yeshe had brushed his lips against the shell of her ear when he'd offered to give her driving lessons. When she'd gasped, he'd probably thought he'd startled her. But no, she'd reacted with surprised pleasure. Her ears had always been sensitive. He couldn't have known it turned her on. Even now, her breasts tightened at the memory of his touch.

When another customer brushed past her, Emma gave her head a mental shake. She didn't have time for this silly attraction to Yeshe. But she looked forward to spending today with him. He'd never know how grateful she was to him for offering her driving lessons, equipping her with a skill for her future independence. That meant everything to Emma.

She plucked a small, local guide to Interior Alaska rivers off the shelf and splurged on a bright pink dry sack and locally made salmon jerky. With her purchases loaded into the sack, she returned to the truck.

Emma spotted Yeshe, leaning against the truck's cab, and paused a moment to admire his large, muscular form. He *was* doing a good job blending in, wearing his hat and hood, eyes covered with sunglasses, and half hidden as he was, near the fence. If people wandered by, they might not see him and certainly wouldn't give him a second glance. Maybe her earlier protectiveness had been unnecessary. But having embraced him, she was now intimately familiar with the sensation of his fur against her skin. Something she was secretively glad to know.

Yeshe pushed off the truck as Emma approached. He didn't look pleased. Was it the droop of his shoulders? The firm line of his mouth? Whatever it was, Emma didn't like to think of him as unhappy. "How did it go?" she asked as she approached. "Is the store going to carry your art?"

Yeshe gave his head a small shake. "No, they're not."

His quiet, defeated tone made her want to murder the person responsible. "Why not?" she asked, irked on his behalf. "Did they—"

He waved a dismissive hand. "It's complicated."

They were practically strangers. So why did she want to make things right for him? "I'd be happy to march into that store and tell the owners about the great opportunity they're missing out on."

That teased a small smile out of Yeshe, which made her feel a fraction better. "Thanks, but no," he said. "I need to let this one go."

With some reluctance, she gave him a nod.

"Here," he said as he dug into his pocket and pulled out a small wooden charm. "One of my carvings. A swallow, like your tattoo. For traveler's luck."

Emma's breath caught as the trinket dangled from Yeshe's hand. People had always considered Gina the traveler, the adventurer—not Emma. She'd never received anything like this and what a coincidence that he'd carved a bird so similar to her ink. Warmth spread through her at Yeshe's thoughtfulness, and that he saw her as someone worthy of such a token.

"I love it," she gushed as she accepted it. "Thank you, Yeshe." An appreciative smile curved her lips as she tightly clutched the swallow in her palm. She'd never received a better gift.

He tipped his head toward her closed hand. "It might also grant you luck during this driving lesson and prevent you from stalling the truck."

She laughed at that. "Really?"

"Probably not, but maybe you'll stall fewer times." He opened the passenger's side door for her. "Don't worry," he said, before closing her in. "Everyone stalls when they're learning to drive a manual."

Although she felt bad that Yeshe's business meeting hadn't ended well, a renewed sense of excitement flowed through Emma thanks to his thoughtfulness. Today she'd master driving a manual transmission, and tomorrow, canoeing on Birch Creek.

YESHE'S CALM, rumbly voice filled the truck's cab. Emma liked it entirely too much. "Put the clutch in and move the stick shift through the gears. Get familiar with where they are. But," Yeshe said, pointing to the worn knob where Emma had rested her hand, "the gears aren't labeled, so picture a double H." He traced the shape in the air explaining where each gear was located. "Move it from first into neutral, the middle of the 'H.'"

Already, this was better than any driving lesson Derek could have given her. The cocky asshole would have mansplained it to her. She'd stayed with him entirely too long. Emma depressed the clutch, then pulled down on the stick shift and popped it into neutral. "Okay, I felt that."

"The stick has play when it's not in gear."

She wiggled the stick. "It's loose," she said. "I've seen this in movies. They take the car out of gear, then roll it off a cliff and watch it explode on the rocks below."

Deep-blue eyes twinkled at her joke. "No cliffs on the edge of this airstrip, thankfully. But that's why you leave it in gear when you park, so it doesn't roll on its own." He nodded at the stick. "Now, shift into second."

Emma pressed the clutch as she gripped the knob, moved it to the left, and pulled down, but it wouldn't slip into gear. She tried again. Nothing, still wiggly neutral. "What am I missing?"

"May I?" Yeshe asked. The back of Emma's seat depressed as he rested his left elbow near her shoulder. His massive right hand gently covered hers on the end of the stick shift.

Emma nearly stopped breathing.

Heat radiated from his palm, and when he lightly squeezed her hand, her breath hitched as she inhaled again.

Had he heard that? Good thing his fingers hadn't grazed her wrist, or he might have realized how his touch made her pulse race.

She didn't want to be attracted to a yeti. Gina made it work, but she lived in Alaska. A yeti couldn't exactly navigate the backstreets of Philly like Yeshe cruised around Wildwood. A yeti didn't fit her lifestyle. Regardless, something about this big, furry guy lit her up.

"Clutch is in?" he asked.

"Yep," she squeaked, then inwardly rolled her eyes. *I need to get ahold of myself.*

He squeezed her hand as he effortlessly guided the stick down. "That's second," he said, his voice close to her ear.

Second? Like second base? The whole scenario

was slightly suggestive. Sweat pricked her forehead and blood thrummed through her veins. *Crap!* She was leaning toward him. Likely because of his weight on the seat back. It had nothing to do with her small crush on the firefighting, woodworking, manual-transmission-teaching yeti. Nothing at all.

"And third?" she asked, her voice a little breathy. What would third base be like with this yeti?

His hand more firmly covered hers as he guided her movement again. "Back up and over until you can feel it catch, then slide it in."

Slide it in.

She heated at his words. Thankfully, Yeshe appeared to be oblivious to the double entendre of his word choice. "And down into fourth," he said, continuing through the gears. "On the far right is fifth gear and reverse. Of course, you'll never actually go from fifth into reverse."

"No, of course not." Emma readily agreed, trying to appear focused. But truthfully, she was more than distracted by his silky fur gently teasing her forearm and how his enormous blue hand flexed over hers. Her summer-tanned fingers barely peeked out from under them.

"Now you try," he said, his touch suddenly gone,

his body no longer hovering at her shoulder but back on his side of the truck.

Emma missed him more than she should have. She should not have missed him at all.

She successfully found all the gears on her own this time, and Yeshe nodded his approval. "Time to start the truck. Clutch in, brake on, then turn 'er over."

Emma did as he instructed, and the truck roared to life.

He beamed. "A-plus."

Emma grinned in return. She couldn't help it. "I thrive on receiving good grades," she confided.

"Mmm . . ." he rumbled. "Good to know."

Her damn breath caught again. Was he flirting with her or teasing? Maybe both?

He continued, focused on the task at hand—teaching her to drive. "Now put it into first, take your right foot off the brake—the truck could roll, but it won't move like an automatic—and give it a little gas as you ease your foot off the clutch."

Emma nodded and did as Yeshe instructed. The truck bucked forward, then stalled. "Fuck."

Yeshe chuckled. "If you'd gotten it on your first try . . . Well, it wouldn't have surprised me, but no one gets it on their first try."

Heat pricked at Emma's cheeks. She wanted to be the exception and didn't like to fail.

"The catch point of each vehicle is different, but you'll get it."

She started the truck again and didn't stall. They were off, clipping along at ten miles per hour.

"Watch the RPMs, revolutions per minute," Yeshe yelled over the truck engine's growing roar as he pointed to a dial on the dash. "Now shift into second."

Emma nibbled her lip. She wanted to get this right. Clutch in, pull down, and . . . no second gear. "Shit."

A firm grip closed over her hand, yanking the stick into second. The engine quieted and Yeshe's hand was gone just as fast as it had moved to cover hers.

"You got it," he said, his voice deep and confident as she increased their speed. When the engine thundered again, he said, "Up into third now."

This time, she shifted on her own. Her eyes focused on the empty airstrip ahead of her, but she didn't miss Yeshe's silent nod of approval that sent her insides soaring.

The engine soon revved high again as they flew

down the grassy, dirt strip. "Now fourth," he directed.

She seamlessly popped the truck into gear and flashed a grin at her companion. "Woo-hoo!"

"Nice job, Emma. You're driving a stick." He squeezed her shoulder with the tips of his fingers. "Now try slowing and downshift. Don't go right for the brake, you need to ease off the gas."

Emma's grin fell as she concentrated. She didn't want to get this wrong in front of Yeshe. She followed his instructions, easing off the gas before shifting into third. It wasn't smooth, but she'd managed it.

"That was great, Emma." Yeshe's fingers teased her shoulder again, sending warmth down her arm. "Move to second gear and pull over. We have company." He gestured out the windshield with his other hand.

When Emma didn't see another vehicle, she realized Yeshe was pointing to the sky. Her stomach dropped. A plane was landing, and she was on the fucking taxiway.

YESHE CRANED his neck to get a better look at the plane. Red with a white stripe and floats. Dale's tail number. "Don't worry," he said to Emma, "The plane will land on the lake. But let's move to the side and you can practice slowing down."

Dale was early. Would he come to Dorje and Gina's party or want to fly to Little Caribou Creek tonight? Normally Yeshe wouldn't mind returning to his cabin ahead of schedule. He'd enjoyed a meal with Dorje and Gina, and attended to his business—not that it had been fruitful. Arctic Whimsy had offered him pennies for his work because he was a yeti. He'd rather walk away than undervalue himself.

Despite this, Yeshe wasn't ready to leave Wildwood yet. Odd . . . His gaze slid to Emma. She had a boyfriend. Plus, relationships complicated life. They weren't for him. Regardless, he wanted to spend more time with her and not rush home.

What was wrong with him? The creek provided fish year-round. The cabin provided endless projects—some frustrating, like a broken stovepipe in the middle of winter, and some rewarding, such as the Dutch door he'd recently completed. He suddenly had the urge to tell Emma about his projects. Ridiculous. What would she care about his two-piece door with hand-carved handles?

He dragged himself out of his head to focus on Emma's driving lesson and the plane on approach. "Look who's killing it," Yeshe cheered, just as Emma braked hard next to a stack of pallets. The truck bucked and stalled.

"Fuck!" She glanced in his direction, grimacing as she made a show of depressing the clutch, putting her foot on the brake, and turning the engine over. "Sorry for my language."

He chuckled and raised his hands. "Doesn't offend me. Nice job getting into second. It's sticky."

Emma leaned over the steering wheel as if trying to see around him. "I thought hiding behind the pallets could prevent the pilot and passengers from seeing us—I mean, keep them from seeing *you*." She gripped his shoulder. "Can you duck?" she asked, as if ready to push his giant, furry self to the floorboards. "Or should I try to drive away?"

Yeshe's lips quirked. Adorable wasn't a word he often used, but the way Emma cared about his safety was just that—adorable. It hit him right behind the ribs. Yeshe gestured to the plane as it buzzed by. "That's Dale," he explained. "He's a private, human pilot and here to pick me up."

Emma stiffened. "Wait. Right now? I thought we were here for my driving lessons." She frowned. "I thought you were coming to the party—I mean . . . It's just . . . I won't know anyone else."

Except her twin and Dorje. Yeshe's heart thumped. *She wants to hang out with me at the party?* "We *are* here for your driving lessons. I wasn't expecting Dale until tomorrow."

She slumped back in her seat. "Right, you don't have your bags or anything. For a second, I thought you meant you were leaving right now."

"I can't leave now, or you'd have to drive home by yourself," he teased.

Emma grew serious. "Up Dorje and Gina's driveway?"

Yeshe grinned. "I like the idea of you driving home. We'll take the back roads. Low traffic and plenty of stop signs. We can switch out at the bottom of the driveway, though."

She narrowed her eyes at him. "Stop signs. You think I'll stall out again?"

"Once you go through all of them, you'll be a pro with the clutch."

"You're testing me."

"Nah, it's good practice," he insisted.

Emma pulled around the pallet, wincing as the truck's gears gnashed against one another.

Yeshe reached over and jammed the stick into

second, loving every moment his hand gripped hers. "Gotta give it some muscle, little bird," he said with a quirk of his lips.

She gave him a sly smile and flexed her biceps. He wanted nothing more than to run appreciative fingers up her arm. "That's it. Show off your paddling guns."

Emma tipped her head back in a full belly laugh that pleased Yeshe more than it should have. The move shifted her hair. She'd pulled it up when they'd arrived at the airstrip. A dark streak of ink lay hidden in the wisps of copper-brown hair at the nape of her neck. "You have another tat," he said, his fingertip brushing over her smooth, warm skin before he realized what he'd done. Emma shivered under his touch, and he quickly withdrew.

Her smile faltered a moment, then slowly grew into something sweet and serene. Yeshe wasn't sure what to make of it, but he liked it. "Another secret," she all but whispered.

"A secret," Yeshe agreed, loving that he now shared two with Emma.

And that decided it for Yeshe. Regardless of the pilot's plans, Yeshe wouldn't leave town tonight. He looked forward to an evening with Emma, even if it came with a crowd of people.

CHAPTER FIVE

Emma had several facades she used when schmoozing with clients, work colleagues, and bosses. She had similar shells she wore when hanging out with Derek and his circle at the country club. But none of those were right for Dorje and Gina's party. The guests and the vibe were . . . different. No smirking red lips that tipped into acidic smiles. People seemed genuinely happy, and real laughter rang in the air. Emma felt like she could be herself for once.

The clothes she'd brought to Alaska were meant for canoeing. In less than twenty-four hours, she'd be hauling them *all* down a river. But she hadn't needed to worry about her casual outfit at the party. Not a single neck held a strand of pearls. Cocktail dresses were absent. Some cute sandals, but no heels. Party-goers sported shorts and T-shirts, and a female yeti named Pema rocked the cutest sundress. If anyone wore makeup, it looked light, natural.

And mixed in with it all was a heck of a lot of snowy-white fur and cornflower-blue skin. Hanging out with two yeti was nothing compared to a deck full of them, making small talk over moose burgers and potato salad.

Fascinating.

But only one yeti held Emma's attention. Yeshe had changed back into his shorts and sporty button-up shirt. Sunglasses concealed his deep, ocean-blue eyes, and he held a neutral expression as he stood, beer in hand, on the fringe of the group. His smile appeared quick enough when someone approached, but it fell equally fast.

"Em," Gina called, wrapping her arm around Emma's shoulder. Gina spun her until she came face to face with another enormous yeti. The yeti beamed and began shaking her hand before Gina had a chance to introduce them. "Tseten, this is my sister, Emma."

Tseten's eager smile and warm, light-blue eyes disarmed her immediately. "Emma, I'm so glad to meet you at last. I've heard so much about you."

She couldn't help but return his smile. His greeting left her feeling welcome and, well, special. Tseten wore a fitted T-shirt with a joke about zeros and ones. While tall and muscular, he wasn't as broad in the shoulders as Yeshe. Emma glanced at her sister, then back at the big yeti, who still cradled her hand in both of his. "Hi, Tseten. You, uh, already know about me?"

He dropped her hand. "I know you're a very successful senior analyst with a corner office back East. You like chocolate chip cookies *with* chocolate chips, unlike your sister. And you and your boyfriend are about to go on a float trip."

All of that was true—except the boyfriend part. But no one at the party knew that. As if to disarm her, the woman next to him said, "Tseten knows something about everyone."

He grinned and shrugged. "I like people."

"I'm Mari, by the way." She gave Emma's hand a quick shake. "Welcome to Alaska."

As Emma nodded her thanks, Gina explained, "Mari is the first friend I made in Wildwood." Gina had been tightlipped about her life in Alaska and, glancing up at Tseten, Emma now knew why. But she had mentioned weekly tea with Mari, likely because she was human.

Tseten cocked his head toward a group chatting near the grill. "Let me introduce you to some folks."

As the gregarious yeti circled Emma around the deck, he shared something thoughtful about each guest. His people skills would be right at home at a corporate event, except Tseten seemed one-hundred percent genuine. However, Emma's gaze kept drifting back to Yeshe, who still stood sentry, lurking at the edge of the party. Finally, she excused herself and joined him.

"Hey," Emma said, as she sidled up to her driving teacher. "You didn't save me," she accused.

His eyebrows rose above his sunglasses. "Save you?" he asked.

"From Tseten. You could have swooped in to pull me away so I wouldn't have to make small talk and could hang out with you instead." She casually leaned back against the deck railing and nudged him with her shoulder, hitting him right above the elbow. "I bet you could have given me the scoop on everyone at the party."

He smiled at that, his lips parting to reveal large, captivating canines, and she felt like she'd won a prize. "But then you wouldn't have met any of them because I wouldn't have paraded you around the deck. That's Tseten's arena. He likes and is good at it."

Emma surveyed the small crowd. "It seems like my sister has a wonderful group of friends, and that comforts me." She paused and shook her head. "So many humans date yeti. Jack and Pema, Tseten and Mari—"

Yeshe cut her off as he huffed a small laugh. "Tseten and Mari aren't dating. She had a nasty breakup a few years ago with a yeti named Nima—no one knows what really happened. And Tseten is in a long-distance relationship with a human work colleague in California named Rosa. Except Rosa has never seen him and doesn't know he's a yeti."

Emma blinked. "He's lying to her?"

"How does he tell her what he really is?" Yeshe countered with a shrug. "If he told her, she probably wouldn't believe him, and if he showed her, she'd think it was a joke or freakout. It's not like he can hop on a plane and explain things to her in person."

And Emma thought she'd had a complicated relationship with Derek. "That's . . . well, kind of sad." Across the deck, Mari now manned the grill by herself while Tseten chatted with a group of people. Emma empathized with them both. Relationships were hard. She glanced up at Yeshe. "What about you? Is there a lucky guy or gal waiting for you back at your cabin?"

Yeshe downed the rest of his beer and shook his head. "No," he finally said. "I'm better off by myself."

Both relief and sadness passed through Emma. Sadness she understood. That sounded plain lonely. But relief? What did she have to feel relieved about? She hardly knew Yeshe. "Why would you think you're better off by yourself?"

He looked at her and paused a beat. "Because then I only have to count on myself."

Had someone disappointed him in the past? Emma rubbed her chest and fought the urge to both hug Yeshe and shove him behind her as if she could shield him from further emotional scarring. Odd. Despite their differences, she'd only felt that sense of protectiveness with her sister. "Whoever hurt you, Yeshe, is my number one enemy."

His lips quirked. "You fight with ghosts?"

What had he meant by that? Were the people—multiple, he had said *ghosts*—no longer alive? Emma crossed her arms, ready to defend her new, furry friend. "I'm up for any challenge."

"Like waking up five hours from now to catch your charter flight?"

Emma blinked at the change in topic. Then she yanked her phone out of her shorts pocket. She glanced at the time and then up at Yeshe. "It's almost midnight."

All he did was smile.

"You're still wearing sunglasses."

Yeshe pushed them up to rest on top of his head. "It *is* getting a little dark for them."

Emma shook her head. "I need to go to bed." But she hesitated, not wanting her time with Yeshe to end. "Will I see you in the morning?"

"At five a.m.?"

She rolled her eyes and launched herself at the big guy, wrapping her arms around him in a hug. "You don't need to get up to say goodbye," she said, allowing herself to melt into muscle and silky fur. Why not? They may never see each other again. On future trips to Alaska, there was no guarantee that Yeshe would also visit Dorje and Gina at the same time. "I enjoyed hanging out with you today. And thank you for the driving lessons. I really appreciate your time and effort."

He grunted and said, "It was nothing," before he relaxed into the hug, his arms sliding more firmly around her. Soft lips brushed her ear, making Emma shiver. "Take care, little bird."

He felt incredible against her. Emma didn't want to let go. Ever.

NO ONE HAD EVER FELT SO RIGHT in Yeshe's arms—or so wrong. Is this what forbidden love felt like? Not love. Lust. Or maybe longing. But why longing? He absolutely did not want an intimate relationship. Plus, Emma had a boyfriend and lived on the other side of the country. Yeshe had only himself and lived alone in the woods by choice.

Still, he released her with reluctance, and she turned to go. "You know what they say?" he asked, trying for a light tone as Tseten approached. "Keep calm and paddle on." So. Lame. Especially if those were Yeshe's last words to her.

Emma grinned as Tseten boomed, "Good one," and clasped Yeshe's shoulder. "Did you make that up?"

"I read it on a T-shirt." The equally lame truth.

Tseten turned to Emma. "Have a great trip and remember to clear your calendar for mid-March." He hooked his thumbs toward his chest. "My birthday party will be epic. You and your boyfriend are invited." He paused before adding, "Unless your boyfriend doesn't know about yeti."

Emma made the sign of zipping her lips shut. "I'll never tell," she promised, crossing a finger over her heart. "Thanks for the invite, Tseten. Nice meeting you. I have an early morning flight—I'm off to bed. Goodnight." She turned away with a small wave.

Yeshe couldn't help but watch her as she crossed the deck to say goodnight to her sister and Dorje before slipping inside. He let out a breath and realized Tseten was watching him.

"That was a big hug for a woman you met today."

Well, they'd actually met last night, but he kept that secret to himself—along with her tattoos. "I taught her to drive Dorje's truck. Stalling a vehicle half a dozen times brings you closer to someone." Why was he making excuses? Tseten could think whatever he wanted. Even so, Yeshe said, "Nothing going on here. I'm not a relationship guy, and she has a boyfriend." Who she apparently had no plans to confide in about yeti. *Huh.* Yeshe appreciated that, the fewer that knew, the better. But what did that say about Emma's relationship if she kept secrets from her boyfriend?

The porch railing creaked as Tseten leaned against it and said, "Emma is different than I expected."

The fur on the back of Yeshe's neck lifted, and he swallowed a growl, ready to defend his new friend. "How so?"

Tseten lifted a shoulder. "Gina had described her as stuffy. Rule following. Timid."

Yeshe's knuckles tightened. "You don't get a corner office if you're timid," he observed as he tried to calm his surge of defensiveness for Emma.

Plus, stuffy people didn't get tattoos. Just how many did Emma have? Images of her bare skin flashed in Yeshe's mind again. He needed to forget that incident. And yet, he knew the curve of Emma's breast would never leave his head. It would likely influence his wood carving. Her plush curves would find their way into his art in many ways.

Yeshe continued, "I've never been in an office building, but it doesn't seem like they hand out promotions and big offices to everyone."

"Good point," Tseten agreed. The corner of his mouth tipped up. "Gina and Emma remind me of my mother and aunt. Sisters can have complicated relationships."

Yeshe rolled his shoulders to relax as he thought

of his late, absent parents. "Any relationship can be challenging, but perhaps the closest are the hardest."

Tseten remained silent for a moment as he looked toward Fireweed Glacier, seemingly lost in thought. "You're right," Tseten finally said. "My birthday might be nine months away, but I love parties and planning them. I want more than anything to invite Rosa to it." Sad eyes met Yeshe's. "I can't."

Tseten faced serious relationship difficulties. His predicament had no easy answer. Another reason not to be romantically involved with anyone. Yeshe would never want to disappoint someone the way his parents had completely failed him, or the way Tseten would inevitably disappoint Rosa. "You're in a difficult situation, Tset."

Tseten gave a silent nod then pushed off the railing and changed the subject. "Helen is non-stop yawning. I'd better get her, Rab, and Dale back to my place." It turned out Dale had arrived early with Helen and Rab so Helen could attend a work meeting in Anchorage, and they could all join the potluck tonight.

Yeshe helped carry leftovers into the house, then he said his goodbyes to the group. He'd have breakfast with Gina and Dorje in the morning, then meet

Dale at the airstrip. As he quietly descended the stairs to the basement, his gaze lingered on Emma's closed bedroom door. He forced himself to keep walking, despite a tendril of longing that tugged at his chest. His time with her had been surprisingly enjoyable. But those short, twenty-four hours of his life were done and over. The sooner he put Emma out of his head, the better. He simply had to figure out how.

Emma jolted awake when her alarm went off. It seemed like she'd only just shut her eyes. She lifted her eye mask and sat up in bed. A wave of nerves swooped through her belly like a flock of birds.

She eyed her gear, organized and ready to go, and a smile spread across her face. The big day had arrived. Emma would prove she could scale the corporate ladder *and* be adventurous—with an appropriate level of planning and safeguards in place.

She dressed and made her bed. Before opening her door, she listened for a moment but heard nothing. Her alarm likely hadn't woken up Yeshe. She was both glad—they'd all gone to bed late—and sad. She wouldn't have minded running into him one more time.

Upstairs, Emma hugged her bleary-eyed sister goodbye, quietly ferried her gear to the driveway, then opened the gate remotely to allow the rideshare to enter. Emma had okayed it with Dorje and Gina—she didn't want to put Dorje or Yeshe at risk by inviting a human to the house without their permission.

The ride to the seaplane base near the Anchorage airport passed quickly. Checking in with the charter flight operator proved simple. She met her very young pilot—he couldn't have been older than twenty—and reunited with her canoe. Before Emma knew it, her float plane roared across the lake, the ground quickly falling away below her.

Despite wearing a headset, she struggled to understand her pilot over the plane's engine. Oh well. Emma was too busy admiring the scenery below on another beautiful summer day. She didn't want to blink and miss something as they flew over snow-covered mountains, lush green valleys, and countless lakes and rivers that reflected the sunlight like silver chains looping across the landscape.

The brilliant-blue sky reminded her of Yeshe's eyes—they were truly extraordinary, and something she *had* to stop thinking about. She'd left him and urban development behind.

With all the gorgeous scenery, the flight passed quickly, and they soon descended toward Little Twin Lake. Birch Creek, which drained from the lake, looked smaller than Emma imagined. But based on her research, she knew flow rates could change dramatically from year to year, over the course of a season, or even after a single rain event.

They bounced once as they came down on the lake, then glided across the surface as if it was a giant water slide. The pilot motored toward the shallow edge, towing into the pebbled shoreline.

In the blink of an eye, Emma stood on the beach surrounded by her gear—multiple dry bags and one canoe that needed assembly. The float plane taxied out to the middle of the lake and took off. The pilot buzzed her, tipping a wing as he flew overhead on his way back to Anchorage.

And just like that, Emma was alone on her ultimate Alaska canoe expedition, the only sound the gentle lap of the lake. She swatted her arm. Then her ear. The back of her neck. A mosquito nearly went up her nose. Right. Not alone then. Accompanied by thousands of voracious, bloodthirsty insects.

Emma dug through a bag and pulled out her bug shirt and hat before pairing her satellite communicator with her phone to update Agnes.

> Emma: Just landed at the headwaters of Birch Creek! It's so beautiful here. I'll check in tomorrow morning.

A return message popped up instantly.

> Agnes: Yay! You're underway . . . Now you have time to send a picture of Dorje.

Emma paused. She had a good excuse to not send anything now but would need to think of a better excuse after her river trip.

> Emma: Can't send photos through my sat comm connection. Setting up camp. Bye!

She powered down her electronics. She'd deal with Agnes and her real life after her trip. But for now, she wanted to focus on the present. Satisfaction hummed through her as she snapped her paddles together and eyed her canoe. After kicking Derek out of her apartment, she'd practiced putting it together in the living room many times, and twice she'd done it with her bug gear on.

Emma deftly assembled the boat from memory while sweating under the sun and amidst the constant buzz of mosquitoes that felt too close for comfort through the clingy netting. All her living room practice and overnight trips with Agnes were paying off.

Anticipating a paddle, she left the canoe near the lake's edge—it wasn't in danger of being washed away—and turned to her gear. Perhaps she should have set up camp first, but assembling the canoe had been exciting.

She chose a flat, sandy spot up the beach, near the outlet of Birch Creek, and pitched her tent. It proved easy to slide the stakes into the sand—no rocks or roots to contend with—but if the wind picked up, they'd pull right out. She found smooth rocks near the creek and placed them on top of the stakes, anchoring her tent and rainfly, just in case.

After carrying her remaining gear to her campsite, Emma rubbed the little swallow Yeshe had given her for luck. Warmth tingled down her limbs. *He believes in me.* He hadn't known about her true plans, but he'd seen her as a traveler, someone capable of adventure. It filled her with confidence.

She carefully attached the carved swallow to her new dry sack. Then Emma strapped on her bright-pink PFD, grabbed her emergency and navigational gear, and headed toward the water's edge. Excitement and adrenaline pulsed through her as she stepped into her boat, then pushed off the shore onto Little Twin Lake for a test run.

As she carved her paddle through the clear, still water, her thoughts returned to Yeshe. He'd be back at his cabin by now on his own remote Alaska stream. Emma paused, water dripping from her paddle. She'd never asked Yeshe if he liked to canoe or kayak. Would it be weird if she asked Gina once she returned? *Hey sis, I have a couple of oddly specific questions about your boyfriend's brother . . .* Yeah. Weird.

Emma gave her head a mental shake and resumed paddling, determined to put Yeshe out of her mind. She was in Alaska and on her own journey.

WHEN YESHE AWOKE the next morning, he couldn't help but peek into Dorje's guestroom. Only a trace of Emma's scent remained—sweet, like summer clover on a cloudless July day. He inhaled deeply, wanting one more reminder of the woman who made him laugh and actually want to attend a party rather than return to the haven of his creek-side retreat.

The flight back to Yeshe's cabin passed quickly. Dale had other passengers to pick up, so he didn't stay. By midafternoon, Yeshe found himself on the shores of Little Caribou Creek. Alone. Again. Why wasn't he sighing in relief like he normally did?

He pictured Emma. Right, that's why. *Damn it.*

To clear his mind, Yeshe took up his grass whip and reclaimed the area around his cabin from knee-high vegetation. The fireweed wasn't blooming yet, but it thrived in the summer heat and had grown taller than the long blades of deep-green grass.

The sun beat down from a clear sky—no lingering haze from wildfire smoke—as he worked the blade. Birds chirped. The creek gurgled and churned over rocks. An idyllic day. So why wasn't he smiling? Would he feel so glum if he hadn't met Emma? Or had life alone on the creek lost its appeal?

He could blame both. He'd been melancholy

before leaving his cabin and had jumped at the opportunity to join the Aurora Crew again. No one wanted a wildland fire, but Yeshe had been glad for the excuse to get out of his head and socialize.

He raked debris and hauled it by wheelbarrow to his compost pile. Next, he cleared a downed tree with his chainsaw, then split the wood for winter storage. With the area around his cabin cleared, he installed a new screen on his Dutch door to keep out mosquitoes and pesky no-see-ums.

As the sun began its slow summer dip for the evening, Yeshe reconnected the water to his outdoor shower. Was it as good as an indoor shower? No. But hot water in his three-sided shower-shed was a luxury at a remote cabin. Despite the day's heat, he planned to use it tonight.

He stripped off his work clothes and plunged into a deep hole in the creek. People paid good money for cold plunges followed by hot soaks. He'd considered a woodstove-heated hot tub but opted for a more versatile shower instead.

Yeshe dunked his head below the surface of the cool creek water and emptied his lungs. He tried to empty his mind too, or at least focus on the here and now. But with his eyes closed, he only saw Emma's flirty smile when she'd flexed her biceps for him. It did things to his heart that he didn't want to admit. He resurfaced, taking in a long breath while slicking wet fur back from his face.

Blinking his eyes open, he viewed his surroundings. Dark, narrow spruce trees lined the creek bank. The low-angled sun shone on a distant ridge. Pillows of clouds built in the eastern sky beyond the ridgeline. *Huh.* Rain would dampen the fire danger and douse the remnants of the Sweetwater Fire, but it might affect Emma's trip. No two ways about it. A soggy canoe trip wasn't as good as a dry one. And if those were thunderstorms . . . Well, lightning strikes wouldn't be good for anyone.

Water sluiced from his fur as he walked from the river to his shower. With a moment of tinkering, hot spray jetted from the showerhead. Yeshe groaned in pleasure. Didn't matter how much fur he had, a hot shower felt great.

After cleaning up, he ate dinner and then sat in his cabin, the top half of his screened door open as a distant cloud bank rumbled with thunder. They were storm clouds, after all. That didn't bode well for the summer's fire season. A dry lightning strike had started the Sweetwater Fire. In the morning, he'd check for messages from his fire crew. They could need him again and Yeshe was oddly okay with the possibility of leaving his sanctuary once more.

He turned a piece of birch wood over in his hands, his carving tools at his side. The sweet curve of Emma's breast moved to the forefront of his mind, and he didn't push it away. He focused on that perfect arc as he plied his knife along the wood's grain and thought of Emma.

After killing approximately one-hundred mosquitos in her tent, Emma finally fell asleep. Turned out that sleeping on a lakeshore hundreds of miles from the nearest convenience store differed from camping at the local state park. First of all, she'd dreamed of yeti . . . Well, one particular yeti. Yeshe's strong furry grip, vibrant eyes, and lush cerulean lips entertained her subconscious in a titillating way.

And second, the sleep wasn't restful, in part because killing the one-hundred mosquitos hadn't happened all at once. She'd smooshed approximately sixty of them when she'd gotten into her tent. The other forty she'd swatted over time—first as she'd curled up with her paper map to plan her first day on the river, and then again as she'd closed her eyes and tried to sleep. Every time she dozed, another fudging bug would buzz near her ear.

It started over again when she woke around two a.m., needing to pee. Staggering from her tent into the brighter than expected twilight of the Alaska summer night had been surreal. No headlamp needed—though she'd packed one just in case. Aside from the bugs, there'd been small noises, sounds she couldn't attribute to other campers. Sounds that made her hyper-alert. Back in her sleeping bag, she'd tucked her bear spray by her pillow—a rolled up fleece jacket—and fell into a restless sleep.

Under partly sunny skies the next morning, Emma sat with her packed gear, ready to push off. She studied her map again as she powered on her sat comm and opened the navigational app on her phone. It was odd. Last night, she hadn't quite been able to reconcile the actual shoreline and river outlet to what she saw on her map.

When the map came up on her phone, none of the waypoints for her planned route appeared. They'd been there in Wildwood, when she'd ensured all her electronics were charged and ready to go. Emma pinched the image on her phone's screen with her fingers. The blue dot indicating her current location looked off. The lake to the east wasn't jellybean-shaped, but it should have been. She would know, she'd been studying maps of the area for months.

Her heart thudded with dread. Was she in the wrong spot? Emma held her breath as she zoomed out. The red dots of her waypoints appeared to the northeast on her screen. She zoomed in and out on her current location and her waypoints.

What. The. Fuck.

The pilot had dropped her off on the wrong lake. He'd landed on "Lower" Twin Lakes, not "Upper" Twin Lakes, according to the labels that appeared and disappeared as she zoomed in and out of the map. Why were there two sets of "Twin Lakes" within twenty miles of each other? Who thought it would be a good idea to give them the same names? And how had she not noticed two sets of lakes? Easy, she'd only focused on the correct lakes throughout her planning.

Emma flew up from the log she'd perched on. She stormed several paces down the rocky beach, her bug net tangling in her face as frustration boiled and a small flutter of panic threatened to creep in.

How had this happened? She'd provided coordinates to the pilot. Her flight reservation included the exact location by name, latitude, and longitude. The

Birch Creek float was popular. It had given Emma a measure of comfort to know others would likely be on the creek at the same time as her.

So, what creek had she been ready to canoe down that morning, and where did it drain? Emma perched on the log once more and pulled up the map, zooming in to her exact location. She adjusted the scale and panned until a label appeared—Little Caribou Creek.

It sounded familiar. She grabbed the guidebook she'd purchased in Wildwood—thankfully she had more to rely on than her map and photocopied description of Birch Creek. Emma flipped through the book until she found Little Caribou Creek.

The description included one line of text: "Navigable but not recommended."

Why not? Where did the creek drain? She panned the creek's twists and turns on her phone screen as it meandered north-northwest—into Big Bear Lake. The lake was big, hence the name. Her scheduled return flight would pick her up at Big Bear Lake in a week at a location between the confluences of Birch and Little Caribou Creek.

Emma had a decision to make. She could message the charter company to demand they pick her ass up and drop her in the correct location. Or she could float Little Caribou Creek.

She was here. Ready to go. Emma didn't want to coordinate another flight from the bank of a remote lake with her limited communication devices and time.

She continued panning the map, zooming in on the creek. Were there beaver dams, rapids, or shallow water? Was it longer than her original float? Her pickup in one week allowed for several extra days. And she'd been practical but generous when packing meals. Her food could easily last ten days. She glanced at the creek. If she wanted to supplement her food supply, she could catch fish.

Who was she kidding? The only fish she'd ever caught had come breaded and pan-fried. Regardless, she didn't have a rod or a fishing license.

She thought about Yeshe handing her the carved swallow charm, and a surge of boldness swept through her. He'd believed in her. Why not give this creek a try? She had skills, gear, and plenty of supplies. If she tipped the boat, she'd rely on her ample emergency kit in the pockets of her PFD, including her satellite communicator, phone, and a portable charger with solar panels. She could request help if worst came to worst. Or if today sucked, she'd backtrack to the lake and contact the charter company for a pickup.

Emma needed to let both Blue Sky and Agnes know about her change in plans. What if the charter company realized their mistake and returned for her after she began floating Little Caribou Creek? Even if they didn't, they would at least have her correct starting location and new itinerary in case of an emergency. Also, she could confirm her pickup at Big Bear Lake.

Emma quickly typed a message to Blue Sky, giving them her updated location, then opened her text string with Agnes. A message waited for her.

> Agnes: My arms are crossed, and I'm tapping my foot. I demand pictures, Em!

Oh boy, she'd have a lot to deal with when she finished her trip. In the meantime, Emma focused on her current predicament and ignored the plea for photo proof of Dorje.

> Emma: Change of plans. I'm on Lower Twin Lake, and I'm going to float Little Caribou Creek to Big Bear Lake.

She included her exact coordinates, then hit send and quickly powered down. She could tell herself it was to conserve battery, but she feared Agnes might try to talk her out of floating a new, unknown creek. However, Emma was determined.

She could do this. Emma took a deep breath and pushed her canoe into the creek before stepping in and nudging it away from the shore with her paddle. And that was it. She was off. With a swell of excitement and pride, she officially started her solo river trip.

FUELED BY EXCITEMENT AND ADRENALINE, Emma made good progress all morning. The creek proved easy to navigate, and she effortlessly cleared the first beaver dam. The second required a multi-trip portage on a lightly used trail. But the trail bolstered her confidence. She hadn't been wrong in assuming she could tackle this creek if others had beat a path into the forest.

Aside from needing to navigate around infrequent beaver lodges, she glided along peacefully. Large spruce trees flanked the creek. Occasionally, the bank rose above the water in rocky outcrops, but muddy or rocky beaches were plentiful.

Clouds began to build around midday, the sun peeking in and out around them. Emma cut in toward shore at a wide beach to eat lunch. She took a seat on a log under a tall spruce tree in the shade and relaxed while she ate salmon jerky and dried fruit. In awe, she watched a sleek, red fox dart in and out of its den dug into a silty bluff above the creek.

Emma might only be a few hours into her trip—and on the wrong creek—but a sense of calm flowed through her. The trip met all her expectations so far.

Several hours later, back on the creek, the fluffy clouds turned dark. Gentle thunder rolled in the distance, and gusts of wind pelted her with dead leaves and sand as it whipped across the creek. Occasional exfoliating scrubs were fun. Eating grit was not. But the timing wasn't bad. Emma's stomach rumbled like the sky. She was ready to stop for dinner and the day, anyway.

She scanned the creek banks for a suitable spot to pitch her tent. Before long, a beach came into view on the other side of a large, rocky dome. She paddled to shore, then towed her canoe up a small beach. Given the narrow beach and steep banks, she tied her boat to a tree as claps of thunder and flashes of lightning moved closer. The meditative storm sound-track quickly grew to a roar, and the sky ominously darkened. Emma needed to move away from the creek and take shelter.

Instead of making two trips, she snatched up all her gear at once, dropping not one, but two bags into the muddy silt before balancing her load. She scrambled up a gully, then into the trees, avoiding the tallest which might act as lightning rods.

She and Agnes had once put up the tent on a gusty afternoon. Well, Emma had pitched the tent. Agnes had watched from the picnic table, since Emma had wanted to practice setting it up without help. She'd do the same today, but after the lightning storm had passed. As thunder boomed and lightning flashed simultaneously, Emma dropped the bag that included her tent with its metal poles before pulling on her rain gear, readying for a potential deluge. She let out a measured breath—this storm would pass—and pulled her PFD back on since it contained much of her emergency gear. Then she sat on a dry sack, reducing her direct contact with the ground. Dried pine needles rained down on her as the branches overhead swayed violently in the wind.

A moment later, a blinding flash lit up the surrounding forest, while a thundering crack made her ears ring. Staying low, Emma spun in time to see the top of a tall spruce tree ignite, flaring like a giant firework. She gasped as the splintered tree popped and snapped, then toppled into another tree. It took mere moments for the second tree's dry needles to spark into flames, then both trees crashed toward the creek. In a deafening groan of splintering wood they fell . . . right across the rope anchoring Emma's boat.

Emma froze, breath caught in her lungs. She dashed toward the shore, heart thundering and adrenaline rocketing through her limbs. Was her boat smashed beneath the wreckage, or had the trees pushed it into the creek when the rope snapped? Both would be horrible. But she only made it a few steps before the downed trees flared with larger flames. A wall of orange heat sent her scrambling backwards.

Shit! Shit! Shit!

Lightning flashed again, this time farther away. But the thunderclap was almost instantaneous. The flames from the downed trees jumped to patches of dried spruce needles and grass. Emma had no choice but to abandon the woods and the search for her canoe. At this point, she'd take the low chance of being struck by lightning over being roasted in a rapidly spreading fire. An image of Yeshe in a yellow, flame-retardant shirt flashed in her mind. He'd tell her to get out of the trees, away from the fire, she was sure of it.

Emma grabbed her gear and backtracked, racing from the trees to a large rocky area that dead-ended against a steep, jagged outcrop. The good news? Little flammable material existed within her immediate vicinity, putting her several hundred feet from the flames, and she still had her emergency gear on her person. The bad news? With the steep granite bluff behind her, the churning creek water nearly twenty feet below her, and smoke from the new fire rolling toward her, Emma was trapped.

WITH WADERS ON, Yeshe stood in the middle of Little Caribou Creek, fishing pole in hand. He reeled in his line, then cast again as he eyed the clouds overhead.

A little rain wouldn't stop him from fishing, and he really needed the excuse to occupy his mind. If he gave it an inch, visions of Emma would take a mile and consume his thoughts.

He'd dreamed about her. She'd been in his bed with him, in his cabin. Laughable. That would never happen. When he'd woken up, he'd had his arm wrapped around a pillow and his dick had dropped, his erection straining against the sheets, eager for Emma's touch.

In previous years, he'd hooked up with a member of the Aurora Crew. She'd shown interest this year, but Yeshe hadn't been into it. The prospect had seemed empty. Nothing wrong with pleasure for pleasure's sake, but it wasn't what he wanted. Perhaps he should have gone for it. Maybe if he had, someone else's girlfriend wouldn't be plaguing his mind.

Thunder sounded in the distance. Yeshe reluctantly abandoned his fishing hole and headed back to his cabin as he watched the storm. Localized light rain was unlikely to prevent lightning-ignited fires in the area. A storm like this had the potential to spark dozens of nearby blazes.

He stepped out of his waders as lightning from the fast-moving storm flashed through dark clouds, thunder rumbling seconds later. Yeshe stood inside the door to his cabin, watching the trees whip in the wind. As they flipped and bent in the gusts, the bright-green leaves on the birch tree by his outdoor shower starkly contrasted against the near purple clouds.

A moment later, a blinding flash lit the area as a bolt of lightning snaked down from the sky, hitting a target upstream. He snatched up his binoculars. A dark plume of smoke curled up from the treetops. Exactly what he'd feared.

Yeshe kept the area around his cabin clear of trees, brush, and other flammable vegetation for this very reason. Every summer brought the threat of wildfire. The cleared area would give his property a better chance of withstanding a wildland fire. But he didn't want to put it to the test. His calloused hands hadn't fully healed from cutting firebreaks for the Sweetwater Fire, but he'd undoubtedly be doing more of the same to protect his cabin. Yeshe had an evening of hard work ahead of him.

He snatched up his Nomex shirt, shoving his arms through the sleeves, pulling it over his T-shirt, then grabbed his pack with his fire gear and first aid kit, and his Pulaski, a wooden handled tool topped with an axe for cutting wood and a hoe for digging soil. But as he darted out of his cabin, a pink dry bag bobbing in the creek caught his attention. An empty canoe followed the bag soon after.

Unless another cryptid had lost their boat, a human traveled Little Caribou Creek. A rare occurrence, but it happened from time to time. Yeshe dropped his pack, his heart thudding. He didn't want to expose the yeti race to an unknowing human, but if they needed help, he wouldn't turn his furry back on them.

He splashed into the water, snatching the bag and canoe. Yeshe pulled the canoe ashore before turning the pink bag in his hands. It looked a lot like the bag Emma had purchased in Wildwood. A sinking sensation pooled in his stomach. Emma wasn't anywhere near here. It couldn't be hers. But when he flipped the bag over, his breath caught. The swallow charm he'd given Emma was attached to the handle.

Blood whooshed through Yeshe's ears. Pink bag, wooden swallow. Emma wasn't supposed to be on his creek. But he'd carved that bird and gifted it to her two days ago. A hundred horrible scenarios flit through his mind, all involving Emma with an over-turned canoe in a lightning storm as a fire bore down on her.

No!

He suddenly didn't care about exposing the yeti secret. He had to ensure Emma's safety. "Emma!" he bellowed as he stashed her bag next to the canoe. No response. At least she was traveling with her boyfriend and a larger party with experienced guides. Only one boat had washed down the creek.

Yeshe scooped up his pack, slung his tool, and took off at a run down the narrow trail along the edge of Little Caribou Creek, toward the plume of smoke and, he hoped, Emma. Trees and other vegetation often blocked views of the creek from the trail, so he alternately called out her name and scanned the water, dashing from the trail to the shoreline and back. His heart hammered as he jumped over logs and smashed through bushes, looking for any sign of a person—or people—along the creek.

More than a mile upstream from his cabin, several spruce trees had fallen into the creek where the previous summer's floodwaters had undercut the bank. The smoke grew thick here, and he still saw no sign of Emma or anyone else. Yeshe closed in on the smoldering ground and crackling trees, snapping and popping as flames licked up their trunks, and called out for Emma again.

A faint sound made him pause. Had someone answered in return?

"Emma," he bellowed.

"Here!" came a shrill voice. "Here!"

Heart pounding like a kettledrum, Yeshe ran from the creek through the trees, along the fire's edge to a higher spot. His breath caught. In the distance, beyond the scorched trees, stood a figure in a bright pink PFD. Emma. Alone and alive, but trapped against a steep, rocky outcrop by smoke and flames. Where was her boyfriend? Her tour guides?

In that moment, Yeshe didn't much care. He focused on Emma's safety. He called her name again, while raising his arms to attract her attention. He could tell the moment she caught sight of him. She jumped up and down, waving her arms. Then she doubled over, as if coughing.

Emma, little bird. His heart clenched. He had to get her out of there. He scanned the area, looking for options. The fire surrounded Emma. He'd need to rescue her from above, climb down the rocky outcrop at her back. If he carried her up the steep side, they'd be able to walk down the backside—as long as the fire didn't move in. But first, Yeshe had to skirt the blaze. Easier said than done as a new tree ignited faster than balled-up newspaper soaked in lighter fluid.

Yeshe ran through the forest. Branches tangled in his fur and whipped him in the face as he raced along the edge of the burning area. The tool hanging from his pack swayed and bumped against him in his rush. The fire extended to a large pond, which acted as a firebreak. He cut left here, circling back to the rocky dome that had Emma trapped.

His lungs burned as he reached the top of the dome. He forced himself to calm his breathing as he dropped his backpack. He couldn't see Emma from the top, but knew she stood more than one-hundred feet below him. The ledge afforded views of the fire's extent and the remnants of the lightning-struck tree, its charred and twisted trunk distinct among the other burned trees. The fire hadn't spread far and produced more smoke than flame. His cabin benefitted, but Emma suffered from poor air quality.

Yeshe dropped over the craggy edge, lowering himself to a narrow, rocky ledge. From there, he carefully downclimbed the cliff face, taking care not to kick loose pebbles down on Emma as he inched along narrow facets. Finally, he positioned himself right above her. He'd struggle to ascend again if he lowered himself any farther. Emma would need to climb to him.

He dropped to his knees, then leaned over the edge. Her lush, mahogany hair came into view mere feet below him. He was so close now. "Emma," he called. "Little bird, I'm up here."

CHAPTER EIGHT

Emma jumped when a deep voice boomed from . . . above her? She spun and looked up. A steady pair of familiar sapphire eyes peeked over the rocky ledge, capturing her gaze. The thundering of her heart seemed louder than the earlier storm. She'd never forget those eyes. But what the heck? "Yeshe?" Of all the people in the world to stumble upon her right now, in the middle of frickin' nowhere . . . Though if she were honest, she wouldn't have chosen anyone else to come to her rescue. His presence immediately calmed her. But what was he doing here?

"Climb up onto that rock," he directed, pointing to her left. "Then give me your hands."

A cough racked Emma's body before she could

respond. "O-okay." Scrambling up the boulder wasn't a problem. She'd already done it once, hoping to climb higher. But no luck.

With a grunt, she hoisted one leg onto the jagged rock. Her palms painfully scraped against the sharp ridges for a second time as she pulled herself up, finally getting first to her knees, then rising to her feet.

Blue fingers reached for her, and Emma rose to her toes to slide her palms into Yeshe's. The moment his large, warm hands closed around hers, a sense of focus settled over her. She no longer heard the cracking fire or roaring creek. Yeshe became her entire world.

"I've got you, little bird," he said as he slid his hands down her forearms. She believed him. "As I pull you up, use your feet and walk up the rock."

Emma nodded, already feeling him tug her up the face of the cliff. She wouldn't allow herself to look down. No good would come of seeing the sharp rocks below or the churning water of Little Caribou Creek from an even greater height.

She focused on using her feet, helping Yeshe lift her up. And in no time, she slid a knee on to the ledge. Yeshe didn't let go as he pulled her all the way up until they both knelt on the rocks, facing each other on the narrow ledge. Emma let out a strained breath as a margin of relief flooded through her. Already the smoke diminished at this height.

Yeshe released her left hand. "I'm going to turn to face the rock wall, Emma. I need you to put your arms around my neck and get on my back."

Emma glanced up at the sheer slab of rock above them and balked. "No way. No way, Yeshe. You can't carry me up this cliff."

Blue lips curled back, exposing large, sharp canines. "I can, and I will." His deep voice was steady, confident.

Although her legs trembled with fear and adrenaline, she trusted Yeshe and believed him. Her gaze locked on his, and she nodded before slowly rising to her feet. Her left hand stayed secure in Yeshe's while he remained on his knees. She slid her right hand around his shoulders, her fingers gliding through silky fur and over his shirt to grip his chest. Then she carefully stepped her right foot around his large body, pivoting and pressing her front into his broad back.

"Okay," she breathed. "Okay." Who was she trying to reassure? Clearly herself. The rock-solid yeti against her chest didn't seem to need it.

"Lean in snug against me, Emma." She pressed

closer, gripping his chest firmly. "I'm going to let go of your left hand. Slide that arm around my shoulder as well. When I stand, bring your knees around my hips and hold on as tight as you can. Alright?"

Emma squeaked another "okay," clinging to the big yeti as he slowly rose to his feet. In all her emergency planning, she had never considered this scenario. A forest fire had ignited right in front of her. The flames had trapped her. And a yeti had come to her rescue, prepared to carry her up a steep rock cliff. A hysterical laugh nearly bubbled out as she considered rewriting her emergency instructions for her next adventure—because despite all this, there would be a next time.

When Yeshe reached up, gripping the rock above them, Emma buried her face in the soft fur of his neck. With her eyes shut, she breathed in his unique smoky scent. Beneath her hands, his pecs bunched and flexed as he made smooth, steady progress up the cliff. Not once did he falter or slip. Soon it felt like he was no longer climbing but striding forward on nearly flat ground.

He tapped her hand, her arm still banded over his chest like a harness. "Emma, we made it. You're safe."

She lifted her face from the crook of his neck and

pried her eyes open. As she did, Yeshe knelt on a completely non-threatening grassy slope several paces from the cliff's edge. Emma released her grip and slid off his back, but her knees buckled as she tried to step away. He swiftly caught her with solid hands on her hips.

"Easy now," he said. He sat her down while he continued to kneel in front of her. "Are you hurt?"

Emma tried to speak, but another coughing fit overtook her. "No," she finally wheezed, trying to gulp in more fresh air now that they were above the smoke. "Just . . . well, that was a lot. The lightning, the fire. It happened so fast. But physically, I'm okay."

He undid the clasps of her PFD and helped slide it off her body. Her rain jacket came next—she hadn't even needed it. Then Yeshe's brawny arms came around Emma, pulling her against his massive chest. She'd been prepared to meet furry, clawed beasts along the creek, but never imagined she'd be so happy to see one. Without hesitation, she threw her arms around his shoulders, overjoyed to be in his arms again.

"Where are the others, Emma? Did you get separated? Where is your boyfriend?"

Oh, fuck. Emma buried her face into Yeshe's

shoulder, breathing him in once more as embarrassment and shame burned her cheeks. Would he judge her poorly for the risks she'd taken and the lies she'd told? The idea of him thinking badly of her churned her stomach, but she had to tell him everything.

EMMA SAT BACK on her heels, digging deep to muster the confidence she'd felt that morning. "I'm alone," she said, swallowing. "I lied to everyone—except my emergency contact. I had a guided trip planned, but it didn't work out . . . and neither did my boyfriend. He's been an ex for several months. I needed this experience to prove something to myself, so I planned my own trip. I kept it from my family to avoid worrying them."

Emma paused, warring with herself. She feared being judged poorly by Yeshe. She'd lied to everyone. But she lifted her chin in defiance lest he dared to challenge her decisions.

She needn't have worried. Yeshe nodded in understanding. "Family is hard, believe me, I know."

No judgment or opposition, only empathy and support. A knot released in Emma's stomach, and her shoulders lowered as they relaxed.

He shook his head, clearly confused. "But why did you choose this creek?"

Emma huffed out a breath. "I didn't. The charter company dropped me at the wrong lake. I'd planned to float Birch Creek." She shrugged. "When I studied my map last night, I was confused. I realized the mistake when I opened my navigational app this morning. My new guidebook said Little Caribou Creek is navigable but not recommended. It didn't look bad on the map, and it also flows to Big Bear Lake, which is where I'm scheduled for a pickup. I've only had one portage. Does it get worse?"

Yeshe's lips tipped into a conspiratorial smile, and a thrill coursed through her. She wanted his secret to be hers, too.

"No," he said, "it's an awesome float. It's shorter than Birch Creek because there are fewer meanders, but it's better."

She cocked her head, confused, but smiling. "Okay . . ."

"The guidebook author is yeti-friendly. That warning and lack of any description is to keep people off *my* creek."

Emma smiled in earnest, realizing now why the creek's name had been familiar. Yeshe hadn't randomly appeared in the middle of nowhere. He lived on the creek. "Yeti remain a secret, and you live undisturbed." Also, Emma's intuition about the creek proved correct. She gave herself a mental high five for trusting her gut.

He nodded, but then his furry white eyebrows creased. "What charter company did you use? It's highly irresponsible of your pilot. Did you contact them?"

"I sent a quick message, but they'll be hearing more from me."

Yeshe took her in again and ran a finger over a tear in her sleeve. "What happened, Emma? I found your pink bag and canoe."

Another flood of relief washed over her. "You did? Oh my gosh, thank you. It all happened so fast. The storm rolled in. I took shelter in the trees, but lightning struck a tall spruce near the creek bank. It burst into flame, crashing down into the creek, and snapping the rope I'd used to tie up my boat. And I didn't even realize I'd dropped a bag." She gestured toward the ledge. "The rest of my gear is at the bottom of the rocks."

Yeshe nodded. "We'll get it, don't worry."

"Was my swallow still attached to the pink bag? Yeshe, I love that charm." She'd put it in her PFD with her emergency gear as soon as she retrieved it. She wanted it on her person for the rest of her trip.

"Yeah, that's how I knew it belonged to you," he said with a small smile. "I was heading to the fire when I found your bag and canoe, and then I began searching for you."

Emma glanced at the fire, realization dawning as worry knotted her stomach. "Does this fire pose a threat to your cabin?"

Yeshe's brows pinched, and he ran a hand across the back of his neck. "As long as the wind stays calm and I get a fire line cut in, I can minimize the risk. It's more than a mile to the cabin. I'll take you there, then come back and construct a break."

Emma blinked. He'd rescued her tonight. The least she could do was help him save his home. "No way, Yeshe. I'm staying right here to help you."

"Emma—" he began, but she cut him off as she unzipped a pocket on her PFD and pulled out an energy bar.

She jumped to her feet, her legs feeling more solid already. "I'm going to eat this. It's even caffeinated," she added, flashing him the wrapper. "And I'll be a new woman." She flexed her biceps and grinned at him. "Remember these? Let's put them to use."

Yeshe grinned in return, his eyes crinkling at the corners and a sharp canine slipping over his lip. Emma's stomach did a happy flip. "Okay, little bird," he said as he hoisted his backpack, wicked looking axe dangling from the holster in back as he settled his load. "Show me what you've got."

As she followed the yeti down the slope and into the woods, she realized that's exactly what she wanted to do, in more ways than one. Today, Emma had deviated so far from her planned trip, she felt like she could write a whole new script. The idea thrilled her. And for once, she wouldn't worry about other people's opinions or how similar her actions might be to her sister. On this trip, Emma would make her own path forward.

CHAPTER NINE

Emma was incredibly resilient. Gina didn't know her sister well if she thought she was timid. Given the absence and indifference of Yeshe's parents, he understood that family relationships were challenging sometimes—or even nonexistent, in his case.

Fire lines needed to be sixteen to eighteen inches wide and all fuel—anything that could burn—had to be removed from the area. Emma worked to clear rotten trees and downed branches, while Yeshe chopped larger pieces of wood and roots with his Pulaski before scraping away dead leaves and pine needles until only a strip of bare soil remained. Thankfully, a light breeze moved the smoke upstream, away from them.

When the first fat drops of rain began to fall, Yeshe and Emma were more than an hour into the effort, closing in on a wet, low area that would provide a natural break. Within several minutes, the sky opened, and it started pouring a heavy, drenching rain. Emma scrambled to pull her rain jacket back on, then dropped to her knees with a laugh, rivulets of rain streaking her soot and dirt-smeared face.

"Mother Nature is giving us a hand," she yelled over the growing roar of the downpour in the forest.

Yeshe leaned on his tool. "It would seem that way. But will it last?"

When the rain intensified, Yeshe ushered Emma under the branches of the closest tree. It wasn't a true shelter. With the rain pounding down, the leaves started dripping on them. He took stock of the smoldering fire. If this heavy rain lasted, it might douse it entirely or at least remove the threat to his cabin.

When Emma shivered, Yeshe's focus moved to her. She needed to warm up, eat dinner, and snuggle into a dry bed. She probably didn't realize it was after ten p.m. He could walk her to his cabin, get her settled, and come back to the fire if needed.

"Emma," he said, placing a hand on her shoulder. She immediately leaned into his side—probably for warmth—but her move pleased him beyond words. "Let's go to my cabin and get a hot shower."

Green eyes, lashes damp with rain, blinked up at him. A slow smile spread across her face, even as she shook again with a chill. He ran his hand down her arm, pulling her snugger against his warmer body. "I didn't realize you had running water. A shower sounds heavenly."

"I don't have running water exactly," he admitted. "But I do have a shower." Yeshe regarded Emma. Rainwater ran from her wet hair down her neck into the soaked collar of her shirt. She'd eaten nothing more than an energy bar since landing on shore. She had to be exhausted. "Let me carry you. You're tired, and it will be faster." That was all true, but Yeshe also wanted Emma in his arms, her curves against his body.

She arched a sculpted eyebrow in question. "Carry me?"

"Like this," he said, scooping her up and holding her to his chest. He loved the feel of her against him.

Emma huffed a laugh but instinctively encircled her arms around his neck, her warm, sweet, clover scent wafting around him, despite the faint smoke smell that likely clung to them both. "Wrap your legs around me, little bird. But watch out for my back-pack and tool."

"I can walk, Yeshe," Emma insisted as she regarded him. But even as she said this, she circled her legs around his hips.

His grip tightened. "I know you can. Do you want me to put you down?"

Her eyes brightened. "No," she responded, her voice deeper, almost husky, and Yeshe's breath caught. "I want you to carry me."

When he'd hugged Emma goodbye back in Wildwood, he'd experienced conflicting emotions. She'd felt both right and wrong in his arms. He'd thought she was forbidden, dating someone else. And now here she was . . . single, unattached, and she'd practically floated to his doorstep.

Tonight, as he marched through the wet forest, a loud, primal voice rumbled through his head. *Mine.* Ridiculous. Emma wasn't his. But still, he fought a pleased growl and lost, his chest vibrating his emotion. He tightened his grip around Emma as he carried her home.

THE HEAVY RAIN only intensified as Yeshe strode toward his cabin. Good. More water drenching the fire meant his focus could shift entirely to the beautiful woman in his arms, whose fingers gently tugged and teased the fur along the back of his neck.

He couldn't have dreamed of this scenario . . . Okay, he *had* dreamed that she'd been in his bed. And now, as he quickly covered the distance back to his cabin, her body pressed against his, his dream came back in full force.

Emma, mahogany hair, flowing like the glossy grain of polished wood, cascading across his pillow. Strong, curvy body tangled in his sheets, tangled with him.

As Yeshe adjusted Emma's weight, his hand sliding across her backside, he let out an involuntary groan.

She tensed.

Fuck, could she hear the sexual undertones in that sound? Pure need. Pure desire. Pure lust.

Emma lifted her head off his shoulder and loosened her legs from around him. "You carried me up a cliff, then worked that wicked tool for an hour and a half. You must be tired." It wasn't a question, but a declaration, and she seemed ready to drop to the ground.

Yeshe didn't relax his grip or break his stride. "My cabin is right ahead and I'm not tired." He ran a hand from her thigh to knee, encouraging her to clench him tight once more.

She peered at him. "But you groaned."

He wouldn't hide his attraction. Emma would be into it, or she wouldn't. And if she said no, then no was no. He'd simply help her continue her trip. But if she said yes . . .

The tangled sheet images were back, erotic scenes of Emma slamming through his mind like a bright slide deck in a darkened room.

Yeshe stepped over a root mass on the trail and pushed aside a branch with wet leaves to prevent them from dripping on her. He could see the cabin, and the shower stood only a few yards away. Reluctantly, he coaxed her legs to unwrap from around him then set her on the ground, his hand lingering on her waist to make sure she had her balance before stepping back. He wanted to give her space before explaining himself.

"I groaned because I'm attracted to you. I liked having you in my arms, feeling you against my body." He glanced down at her hands, loosely hanging by her sides. "The way you wove your fingers through the fur at the back of my neck sent a thrill through me and I couldn't keep it in."

Her fingers flexed, as if in response to what he'd said. He lifted his gaze to her face to gauge her reaction. Wide eyes took him in, pink lips slightly parted. Was she offended? Shocked? "I don't want to make you uncomfortable. If you're not interested, just say so."

Emma blinked. Her throat worked in a swallow. "I didn't want to be," she began after a moment, her voice wavering with vulnerability. "I mean, I didn't want to be attracted to you. All my life, I've tried to set myself apart from my sister."

Yeshe let out a breath, understanding dawning. "And your sister discovered and moved in with a yeti."

She gave a vigorous nod. "But I've also never been to Europe because Gina traveled the continent. And I hesitated to come to Alaska. But Alaska was my dream destination at one point."

"And then Gina moved to Alaska." He hesitated a moment before adding, "But you did come."

Her eyes flashed, and Emma took a step toward him. "I've always assumed I have better judgment than Gina. She does whatever she wants without thinking about the consequences. I don't. I plan. I deliberate. And then I usually make choices I think will please others. But as a result, I'm . . ." She shook her head. "I'm not happy."

Yeshe wanted to do anything and everything to remedy that. "What would make you happy?"

"Right at this very moment?" Emma's gaze moved to his mouth, and his pulse quickened. "Kissing you."

Fuck, yes! A growl worked its way up Yeshe's throat. "I'd be glad to help you with that," he said, dropping his heavy pack and tool before scooping Emma back into his arms. This time, *she* groaned as her legs slid around his middle. He walked forward several paces until her back hit the wood-slatted wall of his outdoor shower. "Emma . . ."

Yeshe paused, savoring the moment of this willing woman in his arms. His heart boomed in his ribcage so loudly it seemed Emma would be able to hear it.

"Yeshe," she breathed, cupping the back of his head, spearing her fingers through his fur. "I've never kissed a yeti."

He gave her a wry look. "I'm glad since you only learned about us two days ago." Then a grin curved his lips. "And don't worry, neither have I."

"But you've kissed humans?" she asked.

He jerked his head in a nod. Right now, he'd give all of them back for the chance to kiss Emma.

"Pity, I'd like to be your first, too."

"You'll be the most memorable," he rumbled in total honesty. "I've known you for two days, and no one has set me on fire the way you do."

Strong arms tugged him toward her plush lips. "That's a lot of pressure," she whispered. "Good thing I excel under pressure." Then her soft, bold mouth claimed his.

Emma tasted of the sweetest summer flowers. The heat from their kiss lit his whole body and made his fur stand on end as they slowly learned each other, lips gently sliding, sucking. The steady rain and damp forest around them fell away, leaving only their growing passion.

When Emma moved her hands from the back of his head to his shoulders, her fingers sliding under the collar of his shirt, Yeshe deepened the kiss. As he swept his tongue against hers, Emma made a soft, encouraging sound that liquified his insides.

He hadn't lied. This was the deepest, most intense kissing he'd ever experienced, and he'd never forget it.

Without the rain and Emma's need for warmth, he could have continued all night. Reluctantly, Yeshe broke the kiss. Emma's glazed eyes and swollen lips nearly undid him. "We need to get you into the shower, not make out against it," he said.

Emma let out a small laugh. "This is your shower?"

"Yes," he said before quickly adding, "I love a good shower." He slowly lowered Emma, her legs sliding from around him before meeting the ground, then took her hand and guided her around the three-sided structure.

"It might be outside," he said, of the shower, "but it's covered, has three walls and a propane water heater. The water pressure is decent." He stuck his head inside. "But I don't have electricity. It's dark in here tonight with these low clouds." He turned to Emma. "I'll get it started, then give you some privacy."

Emma didn't release his hand. Instead, she slowly rubbed her thumb across the fur on the inside of his wrist. He fought a shiver of pleasure.

"It would make me happy if you showered with me," she said.

He took a shaky breath. Naked in the shower with Emma? He swallowed. Gods, yes. His voice came out in a deep baritone as he slid his free hand around her waist, yanking her closer and asking,

"What else would make you happy, Emma?" He certainly knew what he'd like to do if it pleased her.

She crushed her plump bottom lip with her teeth, then said, "Pursuing this attraction between us while I'm here will make me happy." Then paused before adding, "What happens on the creek stays on the creek?"

Yeshe blinked. Quench this desire for Emma and not worry about relationship complications down the road? Those parameters were perfect for him. So why was he a little disappointed that this would be temporary? It was exactly what he wanted. He quickly shook off the stray feelings. His lips tipped up into a smile before he said, "One more reason to love this creek."

Yeshe scooped Emma back into his arms, loving her squeal of delight. Wet clothes never came off so fast.

CHAPTER TEN

Emma had thrown caution to the wind. She was in Alaska on a solo canoe trip, and Yeshe had rescued her from a wildfire. She could kiss and get naked with this yeti if she wanted to.

She'd forgotten any concerns about the future, responsibilities, others' judgments, or comparisons to her sister the moment her lips met Yeshe's.

Emma couldn't deny her attraction to Yeshe. Rubbing her naked self along all seven feet of his furry, muscular body sounded like an excellent plan. The pure masculine vibes emanating from him curled around her like a potent aphrodisiac. She'd give in to her urges with no regrets.

Fully divested of her smoky, soggy clothes, Emma stepped into the steamy shower and the welcoming hot spray. Her skin prickled with sweet anticipation. Large, pointy teeth gleamed in the low light as Yeshe advanced on her in the dark space, a positively predatory look on his blue face.

As she'd imagined, Yeshe's arctic-white fur didn't stop at his waistband. Despite his lush head to toe pelt, she caught a glimpse of flexing abs, powerful quads, and biceps that made her hum in appreciation. The azure of his skin and ripple of his muscles caused patches of fur to appear nearly cyan in color, like foam on the sea. A Hemsworth body covered in luxurious, silky fur. She couldn't wait to get her hands on him.

"Emma," he growled, his smoldering gaze sweeping up her body as she stood completely bare before him. His perusal did more to heat her skin than the water. "Gorgeous," he rumbled, not breaking eye contact as he reached for a bar of soap.

A woodsy scent filled the shower as Yeshe worked a creamy lather between his indigo palms. Perfumed steam, both invigorating and relaxing, wafted around them. When Emma closed her eyes and breathed deeply, she could imagine a green forest sliding by while she sliced through the water in her canoe. "That smells lovely."

"Birch soap," he said. "Neighbor makes it."

Her stomach tightened. Neighbors? This shower had no door. She peered out of the structure. "Do we have an audience?"

"Twenty miles away."

Right. The Alaskan definition of "neighbor." She gave an inward shrug. They would be neighbors if they were the closest people to him.

Yeshe gestured toward her body with the soap. "May I?" he asked.

Have a gorgeous yeti rub her body clean with locally made soap? Yes. Please. She gave him a playful nod. "That would make me happy." He murmured his approval, and her skin flushed with goosebumps, excited for his touch.

She thought he'd start with her chest, go right for the boobs. Didn't all men? Not Yeshe. He turned her away from him, giant hands starting with her shoulders, rubbing small circles, kneading tight paddling muscles, muscles she'd used to clear the firebreak. He knew where she'd be sore. His insight and thoughtfulness warmed her from the inside out.

"Mmmm . . . Yeshe," she purred, bracing her forearms against the shower wall. He worked down her back, the cheeks of her ass, soap slipping, teasing right down her crack only to be followed a moment later by the fleeting brush of his fingers in a move that sent a thrill through her body.

A soapy finger circled the tattoo at the base of her spine. "More ink, little bird. "I want to see this in the daylight tomorrow," he said, his voice low and sexy. Then he whispered his next words, lips brushing her ear. "Do you promise I can explore you? All of you?"

She shivered and her nipples contracted into tight buds in anticipation. "I promise," she breathed, already excited for tomorrow, for someone besides her tattoo artist to see her art.

He carefully scrubbed her legs, both front and back, leaving nothing untouched from her thighs to between her toes. His thoroughness was sexy and so incredibly sweet.

While she rinsed, he quickly lathered his own body. "No fair," she cried.

Blue lips tipped up. "You can wash me another time. But I want to be clean for what comes next."

Warmth pooled low in her abdomen as she ached for more of his touch. She'd be in for a treat if he paid half as much attention to her front as he'd done her back.

As he finished scrubbing, she quickly washed her hair. After she rinsed, a solid wall of hot muscle met her back, and Yeshe drew her against him. She ran a hand down the arm that bound her. Her fingers glided over his wet fur in a surprisingly appealing way.

Lush lips nipped her ear. She gasped, a thrill shooting through her body as his steamy breath teased, and he whispered, "Time for your front, Emma." Yeshe lay sudsy palms flat against her collar bone, rubbing and stroking his way down until he finally grasped her breasts. He kneaded aching flesh, his blue hands and dark, trim claws, filed down to resemble fingernails, were a stark contrast to her pale skin as they sent fissions of pleasure through her. *I have never been touched so well.*

She relaxed into him, breath hitching when his hard length pressed against her lower back and his calloused fingers brought her nipples to stiff peaks. As he swirled the soap over each breast, cupping and squeezing, his giant yeti dick felt even harder and bigger against her back.

Yeshe's hands moved lower, slipping over her belly, sliding toward the part of her that ached the most for his touch. Emma nearly came when his large hand dipped between her thighs, wedging them apart, while his other hand slid over her mound and throbbing, needy parts.

As the soap washed into the drain, Yeshe returned one hand to her breast while the other pressed against her slick, wet slit. When he brushed over her clit, her knees nearly buckled in pleasure. The vibrations from his responding growl passed from the top of her head to her toes as he held her in that possessive grip against his body. "You like this, little bird?"

Like it? Nothing has ever felt better. Emma whimpered as she pressed back into him, trying to get as much contact with his body as she could. "Fuck, yes," she panted as his finger dipped lower and slid inside her.

"I'm going to fill you up." His promise sent a shiver through her body, and when a second, giant yeti finger joined the first, Emma fought to keep her head from falling back against Yeshe's chest. Instead, she glanced down to watch his massive cobalt hand working her pussy, and his two dark fingers thrusting in and out of her. Her body came alive with the sweet pressure, the stretch of him as he pumped into her.

Nothing had ever been so hot. Nothing. It took her breath away.

Emma's legs shook with pleasure, but she wanted more. She wanted Yeshe's dick, its tempting heat pulsing at her back. She reached behind her to grip his solid, furry ass cheek. "I need you inside me, Yeshe."

When his large, sharp teeth grazed her ear, a tremor passed through her. "Little bird," he said, pushing his fingers deeper into her pussy. "I am inside you."

He wasn't wrong, but she wanted more. Emma released his backside and brought her hand around to grip his hard length, his heat pulsing under her palm. "This," she said. "I need this."

Yeshe brushed at her clit with his thumb, making stars appear before her eyes. "I don't have any condoms."

Emma worked her hand up his impressive length, as much as her position would allow. "I have an IUD. And I tested clean after Derek." She tilted her head back to look up at him. "We broke up in March but hadn't had sex in months."

Yeshe stilled. "It's been over a year for me, and I've never had sex without a condom." He paused, and she could tell he'd forced a swallow as he tightened his grip around her. "You want me bare?"

I'll be his first after all. Her chest swelled, and a rush of arousal slicked the fingers buried inside her. "Yes, Yeshe. Oh my god . . . Please, now"

Before Emma could suck in another breath, Yeshe removed his fingers, spun her around, and lifted her into his arms, her breasts rubbing against his chest's solid muscle and smooth, wet fur. A delightful sensation she wanted to repeat again and again.

Full lips devoured her mouth. She didn't shy away but met every thrust of his tongue with her own. She cupped Yeshe's cheeks, rubbing the pads of her thumbs against his coarse jawline, as she ground herself against his hot length.

He notched the crown of his cock at her entrance. "This is what you want?"

She nipped at his lower lip with her comparably small teeth. "Yes," she panted, angling her hips, trying to get more than his tip.

With a primal growl, Yeshe plunged deep into Emma. Her back hit the shower's wall as she gasped in pleasure, completely filled by her yeti.

YESHE COULDN'T HOLD BACK. He thrust deep into Emma's welcoming body. The blissful gasp she let out nearly undid him. He'd never been with anyone like this. Sex had always been quick, more about fulfilling the body's urges and moving on. His few partners had always gotten what they wanted—a big blue cock and a furry body to cling to while they came.

But Emma . . . sweet summer snow. He'd never been bare inside a woman. Her slick heat gripped his dick as if she were made for him. He wanted to pleasure her, wanted this to be as good for her as it was for him.

"I'm not hurting you, am I?" he asked, his cock buried deep in Emma's heat.

Water dripped down her face, rolling between her breasts as she shook her head. "No, you feel so good, so . . . Perfect." She tugged him down for a bruising kiss.

Encouraged by her words and actions, Yeshe pulled back and thrust into her once more, causing Emma to collapse back against the wall with a pleased groan that made his chest swell. She liked what he was doing.

He drove in and out of her body, increasing his speed with each push of his hips. Her hands seemed to be everywhere, caressing his chest, gripping his shoulders, running down the thick fur on his arms.

He reached between their bodies as he pumped

into her, finding her clit, and gently squeezed it between his thumb and forefinger.

She cried out, her fingers digging into his shoulder. "Oh, my god, Yeshe."

"Good?" he asked, already knowing the answer. Her half-lidded eyes and the perfect way her mouth opened as she cried her pleasure told him all he needed to know.

"The best," she panted. "Ever." Her legs braced against his sides as she used his body for leverage, moving with him as he snapped his hips in quick, deep thrusts. She dropped her head to his shoulder, her hands moving from his arms to his chest. "I'm so close. More. Harder."

Gods. He was happy to comply. The soap and shampoo containers shook, rocked, and then fell to the ground as he pounded into Emma, encouraged by her heightening gasps.

"I'm going to come," she moaned into his shoulder, her arms gripping him with more strength than he would have thought possible given everything she'd been through that day.

When she clenched around his cock and shouted his name with her release, his muscles tensed. With a roar, Yeshe thrust deeply into Emma once, twice, three times as he broke apart. A second tremor of pleasure passed through him, knowing he'd come inside her. No barrier, no condom. She'd asked for him bare, and he'd filled her completely.

Panting and still sheathed deep in Emma, he gripped her, cradling her body to his chest as he ran soothing hands up and down her back. "Emma," he whispered. How could he tell her how special she was to him? That he'd never forget this moment. Never forget her.

She carded her fingers through his fur. "Yeshe," she whispered back before sucking in a deep breath.

Braced in his arms, her chest rose and fell against his. "I didn't know it could feel that good," she purred.

Yeshe inwardly growled, proud to bring her such pleasure but angry that she'd never experienced it before. "Same, Emma. That was the best . . ." he paused, reconsidering his words. "You," he clarified, "are the best I've ever had." Sex had never been like this with anyone else.

Small, lush lips pelted his face in a flutter of eager kisses even as his dick slipped out of her. Emma immediately pulled back, squirming in his arms. "I'm going to get you all messy."

Confused, Yeshe looked down to see the fluid leaking from between Emma's thighs. *Fuck.* This is what happened without a condom. His dick threatened to harden again. "Emma," he groaned, dipping his fingers between their bodies. His release mixed with her arousal. So incredibly hot. And when his finger brushed against her clit, and she shuddered, he couldn't stop himself from doing it again. She remained swollen and gushing.

When he dipped his fingertips inside her, then slid them across her clit, she let out a breathy sigh of pleasure—a happy sound. "Come for me again, Emma," he demanded, working her now in earnest.

She shook her head. "I can't—I . . ." Her protests tapered off with a moan. "I've never," she panted, her eyelids falling again. "Oh my god," she cried, her body now writhing against his fingers, her legs once more clenched around him like she'd fall to her death if she let go. Slickness coated his hand as he worked her bundle of nerves, coaxing another orgasm from her body.

Emma jerked against him, burying her face into his shoulder as she cried out. Then she mumbled, "Fuck, yes," into his fur before biting him.

He groaned at the sensation of the tiny bite, a little sting on his shoulder as Emma shook with pleasure in his arms. "Best. Sex. Ever." He agreed, slipping his hand from between her legs.

Emma huffed a laugh. "I'm the one who came twice."

He growled for real this time, nuzzling into her neck. "Watching you come apart on my cock, on my hand smeared with my cum . . . Emma . . . Nothing has ever compared."

Deep down, Yeshe knew nothing ever would. Women like Emma were once in a lifetime, and even more rare for a yeti. He'd savor however long they had together on the creek, live every moment to the fullest.

CHAPTER ELEVEN

A mass of fur-covered muscle enveloped Emma's naked body. Spooning with a yeti—so delicious. Yeshe breathed softly, the giant monster completely relaxed and at peace. She smiled. Yeshe was no beast, no matter how much muscle and fur he had. His heart was pure gold. And his dick? *Whoa.*

Emma squeezed her thighs together at the thought of last night's sexcapades in the outdoor shower. Eight hours later, she still glowed from her first-ever back-to-back orgasms. Or had it been longer? She glanced out the curtainless window above the bed at the overcast sky. At least the continued rain would help extinguish the fire. But who the heck could tell the time in the middle of an Alaska summer?

Though loathe to leave Yeshe's arms, nature called. Emma slid out of his warm embrace and padded over to his "bathroom." He'd retrofitted the original one-room cabin with a closet-sized area that included a composting toilet. Much better than an outhouse or the woods—which is where she would have been had Yeshe not rescued her last night.

She shivered at the thought. The rain likely would have allowed her to cross the narrow, burned area, but her canoe would have been long gone. Emma might have needed to enact one of her emergency plans if Yeshe hadn't come to her rescue.

Before crawling back into bed, Emma ducked under a rope that held her drying clothes. Yeshe had helped her wash them last night after they'd showered. She retrieved her sat comm and phone from the pocket of her PFD, stowed across the room on the wide bench that doubled as an unused guest bed.

As she turned on the devices, nerves wriggled in her stomach. Would Agnes be as supportive as Yeshe about her decision to float a new creek?

Agnes: Okay. I have no idea if that's like planning to hike the Pacific Crest Trail and doing the Appalachian Trail instead, but I trust your judgment. Be safe.

Emma smiled at her friend's encouraging response, and her nerves immediately settled.

> Emma: Not quite so drastic. All is well here.

She stared at the message. Should she say more? But Agnes might worry if she mentioned the fire or losing her canoe and she couldn't find out about yeti. Best not to mention anything else. Emma hit send, then read an apology message from Blue Sky. She reconfirmed her pickup date and location with them before turning off her devices.

She skirted the black stove near the middle of the cabin—Yeshe said it did triple duty in winter as a heat source, oven, and stovetop—and stepped into the kitchen area to get a drink of water.

His small countertop included a sink, but no running water. Instead, a hose with a spigot led to a large jug of water atop an upper cabinet and a plastic five-gallon bucket sat under the sink's drain. Pretty ingenious—though the idea of hauling and dumping a slop bucket sounded way more involved than taking garbage to her apartment's trash chute.

She filled a glass from the spigot and admired his handmade cabinets as she drank her water. Each cabinet door included an ornately carved knob shaped like different Alaska mammals, from whales to bears. Yeshe was *so* incredibly imaginative and talented. All his carvings were amazing, but she loved his bed frame the most. Alaska flora and fauna —all manner of birds, insects, animals, flowers, leaves, and berries—wound around the posts and headboard.

She studied it as she slid back into bed. The more she stared at it, the more detail she discovered. And the more it said about Yeshe, the firefighting yeti who lived alone on a creek. He might be quiet, but he clearly observed a ton, picking up on so much detail around him. It left her in awe of her new friend.

Emma snuggled into Yeshe, her backside into his front. She wove her fingers through the fur on the arm that immediately wrapped around her.

He stirred, his body stiffening a moment before relaxing again. "This is nice," he rumbled then his warm lips kissed the hollow between her shoulder blades, sending a sweet spray of goosebumps down her back.

"Good morning," she murmured, then paused. "It is morning, right?" She'd forgotten to check the time when she'd messaged Agnes.

Yeshe let out a deep chuckle. "Yes, little bird."

His lips brushed over her temple. "Good morning. Did you sleep well?"

"Like a rock," she admitted as she turned to face him, wiggling into his soft fur. It teased her legs, tantalizingly swept across her middle, and drifted across her bare breasts. Emma released a contented sigh.

He lifted onto his elbow then ran his fingers down her arm, a look of concern on his face. "How are you feeling this morning? Any soreness or aches and pains from canoeing, climbing, or cutting in the fire line?"

None of her past partners had ever looked at her that way. Like she was special. Precious even. Emma's eyes suddenly stung as tears threatened. How ridiculous. Flings shouldn't evoke such strong emotions. She rolled her shoulder. "I'm a little sore," she admitted, "but it's not bad." She loved how he continued to caress her, gentle fingers moving from her arm, up her shoulder before he brushed a strand of hair away from her face.

"Do you want to stay here again tonight? When we collect your gear, I can carry your canoe and my packraft. We can float back down the creek together." He paused, his fingers cupping her jaw. "You shouldn't miss any of the creek."

Emma sat up, excitement coursing through her for several reasons. She'd get to spend another day—and night—with Yeshe *and* go boating with him. "You have a packraft? I've read about them. And yes, I'd love your company, Yeshe."

She gazed into those deep-blue eyes and considered additional options. "If you're free, you could float all the way to Big Bear Lake with me." Her heart wasn't set on a solo trip, it's simply how her plans had worked out.

His hand stilled, palm resting on her upper arm. "You want me to come with you?"

Emma ducked her head. "I can continue by myself, but I'd love to spend more time with you." It made her pulse quicken to speak so truthfully, to be so vulnerable.

Yeshe's throat worked with a swallow as he seemed to consider. "Okay," he said, "but I'll need to check in with my fire crew. Yesterday's storm likely spawned other new fires, and they may need me."

Emma nodded in understanding. She was familiar with work commitments—though hers had never included risk to life or property. Still, a ripple of excitement coursed through her at the possibility of spending even more time with Yeshe and exploring Alaska by his side. But . . . "How would you return from the lake?"

"I can hike back from Big Bear Lake," Yeshe explained. "I do it several times each summer. I have a trail up and over the ridge."

She laughed. "Right, you'll jog up and over a mountain with a deflated boat on your back. Piece of cake." Given the way he'd scaled the cliff yesterday with her clinging to his back, it probably *would* be a walk in the park for him, so to speak.

"I enjoy it," he said with a shrug before trailing his fingers along her shoulder. "It's still raining. Why don't we take our time this morning?" He gently raised her arm over her head and dropped a soft kiss on her inked bird with his lush blue lips, then ran his tongue along the swell of her breast. A full-body shiver of pleasure ran through her. "I've seen this," he admitted. "Every time I close my eyes."

Her eyes met his. "My bird?"

His slow smile made her pulse quicken. "Yes, but I was referring to the curve of your breast. The tantalizing hint you exposed in the bathroom at Dorje and Gina's."

Under his heated gaze, her nipple tightened into a hard bud for him, and she nearly whimpered. *How did I get so lucky?*

"I see that curve in everything now—the rounded bottom of a birch leaf, the swoop of a chickadee's plump body. And I want to carve it." He huffed a laugh. "Plenty of artists are known for their sexual innuendo. This arc, this promise," he said as he ghosted a finger over her curve again, "will be in my next carving."

Emma was at a loss for words. She'd never been anyone's muse or the subject of their unwavering attention. Her heart pounded as his admission settled over her.

Tilting her head, Yeshe gently brushed her hair aside, revealing a tattoo at her hairline. "You said that no one knew about your ink. Is that true? Not even your ex?"

A swallow stuck in her throat. Ugh, the embarrassment of dating someone who'd cared so little for her he'd never noticed. "Yes," she whispered, pulse jumping as she admitted the truth. "You're the only person who knows."

A low, dangerous growl rumbled out of Yeshe. "A fool, your ex," he said, a menacing edge to his voice. She pictured Yeshe raking untrim claws down Derek's Porsche and fought a grin at the thought. But then the pad of Yeshe's finger tickled the back of her neck, and she practically purred.

"I see you, Emma, and I intend to slowly explore every inch of your body and find all your ink. You promised I could."

Once again, Emma had to blink back tears. She'd never felt seen by Derek or anyone, not even her family, not truly. She'd mastered the art of appearing the way she thought others wanted, rarely being true to herself. How did Yeshe get that? How did he know her so well after such little time?

She brushed away a stray tear. *Holy shit. Yeshe is too good to be true.* A few days with Yeshe, no strings attached, were going to be the best days of her life.

YESHE HAD WOKEN to a woman in his bed. He was no virgin, but had he actually *slept* with anyone? No. Not once. He'd never even had a lover at his cabin. No denying it. Waking up with Emma was one of the best experiences of his life so far. He wanted to do it again. And again. A disturbing thought given their temporary arrangement.

But Emma needed someone to *see* her, and Yeshe wanted to be that person, despite their limited time. He knew too well what it was like to feel invisible. He planned to run his fingers over every inch of her body. Not only did he want Emma to know he saw her, but he was also greedy. The pleasure he'd get from learning her inside and out created a new sensation right behind his ribs. A scary sensation, and yet he had to feed it.

He caged Emma's body with his own before gently sweeping her hair away from the nape of her elegant neck. He ran a finger over a mark he didn't recognize. "What's this?" he asked.

"Gemini," she said, adjusting the pillow under her head so it didn't muffle her voice. "It's the astrological sign."

Yeshe traced it again. "Twins. I haven't known your sister long, but I think she'd get a matching tattoo in a heartbeat." They might have their differences, but this was clearly a sign of love and devotion toward her sister.

Emma's lips curved up. "Maybe. But in color."

"This suits you," he said.

"Boring and practical?" she asked, amusement in her voice.

"Classic simplicity. Don't underestimate its power. Less is often more."

He watched her throat work with a swallow as his gaze tracked back to the ink by her breast. "Tell me about this," he said, lifting her arm above her head as he rolled her onto her back.

Emma glanced down to where he traced the art. "A swallow. There isn't a story behind it."

"Little bird," he rumbled. "Sometimes our subconscious takes over. This is you. Flexing your wings. Soaring high. Free from your burdens. Free to make your own choices."

Emma made a choking sound, eyes swimming with liquid. "I don't . . ."

He pressed his lips to hers in a soft kiss. "I'm telling you my interpretation. Read into it what you will." Swallows nested along the creek's bank. They would forever remind him of Emma now.

With a slow tug on the sheet, he exposed her stomach and kissed his way down to her hips, where he found another small work of art. "A rose."

"My grandmother loved her roses," Emma explained. "They look fragile, but they hold up to a rainstorm better than a lot of flowers and come back year after year."

Yeshe brushed his lips across the small bloom. "Strength and perseverance."

She gave him a wry smile. "And I can hide it behind the band of my underwear."

Like from her boyfriend. Anger simmered on her

behalf, but he flashed a devilish grin, one he knew bared his large teeth. "You're not wearing underwear."

He swirled his tongue around the flower, then licked his way down the crease where her leg met her hip, shuttering when he caught the sweet, enticing scent of her arousal. Yeshe yanked the sheet off Emma's lower half and wedged his large body between her legs, spreading them wide.

Her hand went to her eyes as sunrise pink crept into her cheeks. "Oh my god, Yeshe. I'm so on display."

"I don't want to miss an inch of you," he growled before lifting her hips and placing a slow kiss on her wet center. "Any ink down here?" he asked before swirling his tongue up her slit and flicking against her clit.

Emma cried out in pleasure before answering him in a husky tone. "No, but now I wish I did." She waved a hand. "Feel free to linger here, anyway."

Yeshe brushed the flat of his tongue across her sensitive flesh once more before moving to her inner thigh. "I'll be back. I promise."

He kissed his way down both legs, lavishing each with attention, but not stopping until he reached her left ankle, where a small star winked up at him.

Emma leaned up on her elbows. "No story. It's a teeny star, easy to conceal. It was my first tattoo, and I got it on a whim one evening after Derek bailed on me for some country club event."

Yeshe growled. "You were too good for him, Emma."

She huffed an unconvincing laugh. "He was an ass, but it still hurts."

He rubbed her leg, wanting to erase her pain. Wanting to be a person she could count on. But a brief tryst didn't work that way. Instead, he focused on her ink. "People have long used stars to guide them," Yeshe declared, cradling her foot against his lap as he kneeled between her legs. "Especially the north star—it's on the state flag."

"North to the future," she said as she pulled her leg from his lap. "The state motto—I read many guidebooks before coming on this trip." Emma knelt before him, her eyes roaming his body like a predator ready for her prey—and he wanted her to devour him.

Her hands whispered over his fur. "I want to explore *you*. You're a lot more interesting."

He swallowed. "I disagree."

Roaming fingers moved lower. "Where's that giant blue dick? Explain this to me."

When firm hands slid between his legs and cupped his balls, he groaned low. He'd had women begging for his dick before, but none had bothered to learn how his body worked. Of course, Emma would.

"My sheath," he explained with a grunt as he guided her hands forward to the furry swell that held his cock, "protects my dick. Yeti were born to run around naked."

"Right," she said, her hands teasing over him. "You don't want all your sensitive bits exposed to harsh elements."

"Mmm . . . And when we get aroused—"

She arched her eyebrow and widened her knees to expose her wet pussy to him. "Like now?"

Fuuuuck. The glistening broad tip of his cock head emerged from his sheath. "Yes," he ground out as his dick swelled and fully dropped, bobbing between their bodies like an eager friend who'd only just arrived at the party.

Both of Emma's small hands wrapped around his shaft. "So soft," she murmured. "And hard." Her hands twisted. "And big." Then she dipped forward, that perfect mouth closing over his crown.

His hands flew to her shoulders. He wasn't sure how much he could take. "Emma," he panted. "I wasn't done exploring you. I know you have a masterpiece right above that perfect ass."

She popped her mouth off his dick in the most provocative way, her lips curving upward. "You like my ass?"

"Fucking love it," he growled before flipping her onto her stomach in one smooth move. With a squeal, she hit the mattress and lay sprawled before him.

"Yeshe," she cried. "No fair. Now I can't see you." She might claim it wasn't fair, but she widened her legs in invitation.

"Oh, but you'll feel me," he promised in a low voice as he brought her to her hands and knees before pressing a kiss to the blazing red sun swirled around her tailbone, the embellishment drawing his eye to her perfectly rounded cheeks. This is what had teased him in the shower last night. "Life," he said. "Energy. Power."

"I got it . . ." she panted as he palmed her ass, "for this trip. The midnight sun."

"All the more reason to celebrate it," he murmured before he spread her cheeks. He placed another wet kiss on the tattoo before he licked his way down her inviting crack leading his tongue to her wet pussy. Then he devoured her.

It wasn't long before Emma broke apart with a hoarse cry. But even as she still writhed against his face, she begged, "I need you, Yeshe."

Who was he to deny her?

As Yeshe rose to his knees behind her, Emma reached between her legs, helping guide him to her entrance. No resistance. His tip blissfully slipped right in.

He fed her more, watching as his blue shaft disappeared into her flush, welcoming body. When his hips kissed her ass, his palms gripping her hips on each side of her fiery sun, they were both panting. "Emma," he growled.

"Give me everything," she demanded. "Don't hold back."

He didn't. Couldn't. With swift, even strokes, heat began to build. He slid a hand between Emma's thighs, rubbing her clit with the pad of his finger while he increased his thrusts, the headboard rhythmically thumping against the wall with each pump of his hips.

Emma clenched around his cock. "Oh, yes," she purred, as her body shook with her climax.

Balls tightening, he quickly followed, bending over Emma and holding her to him as his cock pulsed and spasmed, releasing deep inside her. Again.

Still sheathed within her, he collapsed to his side, bringing Emma with him. His chest rose and fell like he'd paddled a mile upstream. He pressed a kiss to Emma's temple. "Amazing," he murmured. He'd never experienced such bliss.

She snuggled into his body. "Together," she said, sounding sleepy already. "We're amazing together."

Awareness pricked over his skin. She wasn't wrong. But what did that mean? They only had a few days, after all.

CHAPTER TWELVE

Romance novels drew inspiration from dicks like Yeshe's. He kept rising to the occasion—literally—for Emma's utter and complete pleasure. His too, if his moans, groans, and sexy growls were any indication.

After a long morning in bed with naps punctuated by sex—or sex punctuated by short naps—Emma woke in Yeshe's arms again, a smile curving her lips. Had she ever woken up smiling before today? Definitely not. She hadn't even known it was possible. Is this what happened to happy people? Because Emma was most definitely happy. Yeshe made her feel so special. He'd not only noticed her tattoos, but made a point to understand them—to understand her. She wanted to slow the clock, savor her time in Alaska, and with Yeshe.

"Mmm . . ." Yeshe hummed a contented sigh, as he pulled her closer to him, making her smile grow wider. "As much as I want to never leave this bed, we should eat and collect your gear. Plus, there's something along the creek I'd like to show you when we float back toward the cabin. A surprise."

Emma grinned. "Surprise? Tell me."

He chuckled. "Now if I did that, it wouldn't be a surprise." He paused, then asked, "Do you like sourdough pancakes?"

Emma's stomach answered for her, rumbling loudly against the large palm that rested against her abdomen. She huffed a laugh. "That's a yes. Sounds delicious. Where did you get your starter?"

"Nana," he said, "Dorje's grandmother."

Emma turned in his arms to face him. She brushed a hand along the smooth fur of his chest, loving the sensation against her skin. "That's like a family heirloom. How special to have a constant reminder of a loved one that literally feeds you, keeps you alive."

Instead of immediately agreeing with her, like she expected, Yeshe's smile slowly fell. "What did I say, Yesh?"

He slowly shook his head. "It's nothing . . ." But clearly it was. "I've simply never thought about it that way." He leaned up on an elbow above her. "Nana treated me like her own grandson, even though we weren't related. She differed greatly from my own parents."

Emma traced a finger along the edge of a wild rose carved into Yeshe's bed frame. "Did one of your parents teach you how to work with wood?"

Yeshe gave a harsh snort, and Emma couldn't help noticing that he'd stiffened. *Crap, I've hit a nerve.* She hadn't intended to.

"No, I picked that up on my own," he said before heaving a weighty sigh. "My parents were absent more than they were present during my childhood. And the few memories I have of my parents aren't good."

Emma wanted to erase the hard look that had crossed Yeshe's face. She slid his hand from her hip to her chest, pressing it against her heart. "Well, you're extremely talented, Yeshe. I've felt like some kind of forest princess sleeping in your bed with this ornately carved headboard. Believe me when I say it's a new feeling for me . . . But I like it. Every time I study the frame, I see something new. As my eyes were fluttering shut with my third—or was it my fourth, orgasm this morning—I found a little frog I hadn't seen before."

His lips curved into a smile, the pain from a moment ago thankfully fading. "Princess? What does that make me?"

She gave him a playful smile and rolled her eyes. "I dunno, but I'm insanely jealous to think about any other woman sleeping in your bed."

His smile fell. "No other woman *has* slept in my bed," he admitted.

Emma tried and failed to hide her victorious smile. She loved being Yeshe's first of anything. "And the shower?"

His deep-blue gaze bore into her with so much intensity she nearly gasped. "I've never had a lover at my cabin. You're the only woman to feel like an . . . um, a princess—."

Oh. She took an uneven breath then softly added, "*Forest* princess."

"Forest princess," he amended, his lips twitching, "in my bed." He placed a soft kiss on her lips.

Emma had never imagined being anyone's princess, yet here she was. Her canoe trip in Alaska had taken her out of her comfort zone yet also been something she'd desperately wanted to do. What other possibilities could she discover if she'd only take the chance?

AS PLANNED, Yeshe carried Emma's canoe upstream. She offered to carry his backpack with his packraft, but a pack sized for a yeti was way too big for her. When they arrived at the burn area, they found soggy, black earth and charred trees and branches.

The heavy overnight rain and steady morning drizzle had extinguished any fire threat. Still, Yeshe left the boats by the creek while he and Emma inspected the scorched area looking for burning stumps or lingering hot spots. They found neither. While the smoke had been pervasive, the wind direction and wet ground to the south limited the size of the burned area.

They retrieved Emma's gear from the base of the granite cliff. Ash coated the sacks, but her extra clothes and provisions weren't damaged and remained dry, despite the current wet conditions.

Previously, Yeshe hadn't given the cliffs much thought. Now they'd always remind him of Emma. His gut clenched at the memory of seeing her trapped against them by the fire, doubled over while coughing from the smoke. He couldn't help but clasp her hand in his, keeping her close as they walked back to the boats.

He needed to check himself. Emma would leave Alaska when she finished paddling the creek. He'd only set himself up for disappointment if he let his mind play "what-if." He'd always been content living by himself. While he'd enjoyed more of Dorje and Gina's company over the last few months, that didn't mean he should consider having a partner of his own.

Soon they were on the water. Yeshe tipped his paddle into the creek and turned his boat toward Emma's canoe. He'd floated Little Caribou Creek with Dorje and Tseten a few times, but mostly he'd been alone on the water. He loved paddling with Emma, and found he wanted to continue beyond their few days together.

"Are we any closer to the surprise?" Emma asked as she turned toward him.

The sun, which had finally made an appearance, backlit her hair, giving her a soft, angelic glow. "Around the next bend," he said. "Stay to the right."

As they floated around the corner, he pushed his paddle through the water and, in two swift strokes, his raft nudged her canoe. He extended a paddle toward her. "Grab this," he instructed as he reached up and wrapped his hand around a spindly willow growing out of a fracture in the rocky bank behind them, holding them in place as the swift current rolled past.

"See the bluff up ahead? It's an old wind-blown silt deposit. Bank swallows burrow into the silt and nest. They come and go from their nests as they feed on insects. These swallows inspired me to carve the little charm I gave you."

Emma watched the bluff, while Yeshe watched Emma.

She let out a small gasp as a bird flew from its burrow, flitted over the creek's surface, then disappeared into the bank again. "When it soared over the water, it looked just like my tattoo and the charm." The wonder in her voice caused an odd, but pleasant, warming sensation across his chest.

He grinned. "Surprise."

When Emma turned toward him, his breath caught. He'd seen looks like that before, but they'd never been directed at him. Adoration, caring . . . Love? No, it couldn't be. Still, that warming sensation radiated from his chest until his limbs tingled with awareness.

"I'd really like to kiss you right now, Yeshe,"

Emma said. "But I don't want to tip my canoe or your raft."

He wanted that, too. Wanted to lay her out on the next sandy beach and make her his, again. "Let's stay dry," he agreed. "But I'll take you up on that kiss the second we hit the shore."

"Deal," she said, before adjusting to face him. "I also recognize these birds from your other carvings. One of your wooden spoons had a swallow on the end."

Yeshe nodded. He'd carved hundreds of spoon variations over the years.

She narrowed her eyes. "But the spoon you used to mix the pancake batter had a fish carved into the handle."

"A salmon," he confirmed.

Emma was quiet for a moment, but appeared deep in thought. Finally, she said, "You didn't go into detail about your meeting with Arctic Whimsy, but I gather it didn't go well."

He blew out a breath. "They offered me pennies. A lot less than they pay other artists I've known."

Emma frowned. "They think they can get away with it because you're a yeti."

He raised an eyebrow. She wasn't wrong.

"Yeshe, may I make some inquiries on your

behalf? The sporting goods store had a locally made section—they even had dry brownie mix from Wildwood Bakery next door. What if they agreed to collaborate and sell a mixing spoon with it as a gift set?"

He gave her a knowing smile. "This is how you earned your corner office."

She rolled her eyes and made a "pfft" sound. "It's overrated. Believe me." She paused a moment. "So . . . what do you say?"

Yeshe had been ready to give up on selling his woodworking in brick-and-mortar stores. It wasn't easy to approach a stranger to sell one's art, and the low-ball offer from Arctic Whimsy had challenged his self-worth. But what did he have to lose if Emma reached out to businesses for him? He'd continue carving for himself either way. "I make bowls too," he added, grinning at her.

She grinned back. "Excellent. I'll take that as a yes. Spoons and bowls to accompany the brownie mix." Her eyes sparkled as the sun reflected off the water, and Yeshe realized he'd likely never been happier. "I think your cabinet handles would do well in other venues." She paused, brows slanted again in that calculating way. "What else have you made?"

"Ornaments, walking sticks, small tables and

stools . . ." His woodshed overflowed with years' worth of projects. "Alaska winters are long," he explained. And he'd spent most of that time alone, with little else to fill his days.

"I'm going to work the 'shy, reclusive, Alaska mountain-man' angle, both for marketing reasons and to give an excuse why businesses may never meet you in person." She splashed the water with her paddle. "Buckle up, Yeshe. This is going to be a fun ride."

It was way too late for safety precautions. The wild ride with Emma had already begun. And it had nothing to do with his carving, and everything to do with her and the heart he'd so carefully protected all these years . . . At least, until now.

CHAPTER THIRTEEN

Sun filtered through Yeshe's window the next morning. As Emma lay in his bed, wrapped in his arms, she was afraid to breathe, to move an inch. Perhaps if she didn't wake him, they could stay like this a little longer . . . Maybe forever.

But why hope for something that could never be? Instead, once Yeshe woke up, she crawled on top of him, soft fur brushing her inner thighs, and rode her yeti in a way she hoped neither of them would ever forget.

Some time later, though it felt like none at all, they'd dressed, consumed another giant stack of sourdough pancakes and were pushing their packed boats into the creek. Similar to yesterday, Yeshe had dressed in quick dry pants and another form-fitting T-shirt. Emma openly stared at his chest, his pecs and biceps bunching and flexing as he deftly maneuvered his packraft around the creek.

As they floated along, he pointed out his favorite spots for berry picking, bird watching, and where he once saw a porcupine fall from a tree. The latter caused Emma to glance up at every tree limb overhanging the creek, though Yeshe assured her they were rare to see and were mostly excellent climbers.

They stopped for a break around midday, and Yeshe led Emma on a short hike to a lake filled with bright green lily pads topped with vibrant yellow flowers. While they ate lunch on a downed log, a bull moose moseyed into the far side of the lake, dipping his large, antlered head into the water to dredge up a lunch of his own.

The afternoon slipped by as they drifted past spruce forest, clumps of brilliant-white paper birch trees, and several small waterfalls cascading into the creek. Emma found the views from the water exactly as she had hoped, and sharing the experience with Yeshe made them even more special.

The sun shone high in the sky, surprising Emma whenever she glanced at the time and saw how many hours had passed. But she still couldn't believe it when her watch read nine-thirty p.m. "Do you know what time it is?" she called out to Yeshe who was ahead of her on the creek.

He looked to the sky and then back at her and lifted a shoulder. "Half-past nine, I'd guess."

Emma slowly shook her head. "How can you even tell?"

He laughed. "It's late June. The sun is lower on the horizon than earlier in the day. It's filtering between the trees now."

"Yes, which means it should be late afternoon or early evening," she protested. "Not nine p.m." She paddled closer to Yeshe. "No wonder I'm hungry."

He nodded downstream as they rounded a bend, and a wide sandy beach came into view. "There's a great camping spot ahead. We'll set up your tent, cook dinner, then hike up this dome and watch the sunset." He motioned to a rocky hill to their right before grinning and adding, "And sunrise."

Emma rested her paddle against the side of her canoe, ready to take his bait. "When is sunset?"

"About one-thirty a.m.," he said casually, as if it were no big deal that it would go down *after* midnight.

"And sunrise?" she asked.

"One forty-five a.m., give or take a few minutes."

Emma shook her head. "Fifteen minutes apart."

Yeshe nodded, his smile contagious, and Emma grinned at him.

"We'll be up all night," she said.

He gestured to the sky. "The beauty of an Alaska summer. It's always light out. It doesn't matter what time it is or what schedule you keep. You can stay up all night, sleep all day, and you'll still have light and sunshine while you paddle along."

All Emma could do was laugh. The concept challenged her, yet it felt oddly freeing too. What did it matter if they were up all night and slept in? The only event on her calendar was her return flight. As long as she caught her charter plane, nothing else mattered.

Yeshe helped her set up her two-person tent on the grassy bank above the beach. "I bought the tent when I thought Derek and I would take the trip together." Emma banged a rock against one of the tent stakes, driving it into the ground. "It's lightweight, and I didn't want to buy a one-person tent until after I tried this one."

She surveyed her work then glanced from the

tent to Yeshe and back. "You're not going to fit in there, are you?"

His eyes twinkled. "I can try."

Yeshe lived up to his word. He tried. Emma lay on her side in the tent next to a very cramped looking yeti, whose legs stuck out the open door. They hadn't bothered with the fly under the cloudless sky. "And the answer to the question, 'how many adult male yeti can you fit into a two-person human tent?' is . . . none. At least, not if you want to zip the tent shut and keep out the mosquitos." She leaned up on an elbow. "I'm sorry, Yeshe. Did you bring a tent?"

"Nah." He swatted at a mosquito, catching, and squishing it in his hand before flicking it outside. "Then I'd have to carry it back."

She eyed the tent door. The zipper was placed about four inches up from the tent's bottom—strategically so, she'd read. The bottom of the tent could get wet and wouldn't flood the inside. But Yeshe's legs pressed the zipper into the ground. She didn't worry about flooding, but comfort. That had to rub against his calves. "Will you be comfortable in here?"

He swatted at another mosquito. "If I stay in here, you're going to get eaten alive with the door open."

Emma frowned, not wanting to sleep in the tent

if Yeshe couldn't. She longed for his bed. "But won't the mosquitoes bother *you* outside?" she asked.

"I'll start a small fire on the beach. The smoke will keep the bugs down. I'll be fine." With a grunt, he partially sat up, his head grazing the top of her tent. "Let's make dinner, then hike up the trail to the overlook for sunset."

Emma tried not to show her disappointment. She wanted to sleep in Yeshe's arms, not in a tent near him. While she busied herself with storing her sleeping bag, mattress pad, and her few spare clothes inside the tent, Yeshe pulled out the stove and heated water for cooking.

She joined him several minutes later, perching on a log he'd rolled onto the beach by their cooking area.

Yeshe wasn't watching the stove, though. His phone had his full attention. He'd pushed his sunglasses onto the top of his head. The crease of his white eyebrows signaled bad news.

Emma turned the stove down as the water had begun to boil. "Is everything okay? Does the fire crew need you?"

Yeshe's gaze met hers, those deep-blue pools looking turbulent. "No, it's a message from Dorje."

He paused, and her gut clenched. That couldn't

be good. Her thoughts flew to her sister. "What's wrong? Is Gina okay?"

He swallowed, then said, "They know you're not with Derek or on the trip with Wild Alaska Outfitters."

Emma's heart stopped, missing several beats. Or maybe it kept beating, but her lungs seized. She wasn't sure. But when she finally sucked in a deep breath, her heart boomed, blood whooshing through her veins.

"Your sister tracked your phone to a location right outside Anchorage."

Fuck. Emma had set up tracking to keep tabs on Gina and all her global wanderings. She *never* imagined the roles would be reversed. And with the app they used, her last location would reflect the moment she left the Anchorage cellular network. Tethering to the sat comm didn't provide the app location information, otherwise they'd know she traveled Yeshe's creek.

"They're asking if I can help search for you if it comes to that."

Emma's stomach roiled, and she instinctively pressed her hands to her middle. She hated causing anyone to worry on her behalf. She did not want to be a burden.

"Can you please tell them I'm safe and relay my return flight details? They'll know that I'm with you and have questions, I'm sure. I'll share all the details with them when I'm back in Anchorage." Her voice sounded as small and as vulnerable as she felt. "I'm so sorry," she whispered as Yeshe tapped out a message.

Emma never imagined her family would discover her true plans in the middle of her trip. What did they think of her now? Or worse, what did Yeshe think of her now?

Lunch had been hours ago, but that didn't stop Emma's stomach from revolting. She jumped up, ran across the beach to the bushes, and puked.

***

AS YESHE HIT SEND ON a message back to Dorje, Emma jumped up and retched into the bushes.

He ached for her. He hadn't known Emma long. But from what he'd observed, she hated causing *anyone* distress, especially her family. And now, her sister and Dorje were out there looking for her, worried, and reaching out to people for help.

Yeshe knelt by her side and handed her a bottle

of water. "Emma," he said, as he brushed her hair away from her face and ran a hand down her back. "It's going to be okay."

"I'm so sorry," she croaked. "I don't usually do things like this. I'm normally much more responsible."

He chuckled. "I know you are. And you don't need to apologize to me."

She blinked at him, eyes red and welling with tears as she rinsed her mouth. "But you must be so disappointed in me."

The ache behind his ribs only intensified. He scooped her into his arms. "Never, Emma. You were in a tough position. I don't blame you. Despite your career success, it seems like you've rarely put yourself first. You finally had the chance to do what *you* wanted. And you were afraid it wouldn't happen if your family knew all the details."

A stray tear ran down her cheek. "I blew it. The pilot left me at the wrong spot. You had to rescue me from a wildfire, of all things. And now your brother and my sister know I lied. I'm not with Derek or on the Arctic River with guides. I wanted a little freedom to do something for myself without causing anyone to worry." She sniffed. "How did they even find out?"

"First of all, the drop-off wasn't your fault. The pilot should have known better. The fire was a freak accident. No one could have predicted that." Yeshe glanced at Dorje's messages on his phone. Emma wouldn't like this next detail. "As for who you're not with, your parents saw Derek on TV, some financial show."

Emma flew out of his lap. "What?"

"They were concerned," he said, continuing. "Since they thought he was in Alaska with you."

She paced a few steps, spearing her fingers through her hair. "My parents know, too?"

He stood and wrapped his arms around her again, wishing he could do more for her. "Look on the bright side. At least you don't have to worry about how you're going to break the news to them."

She huffed a watery laugh against his chest. "I don't know if that's good or bad."

"It is what it is," he said. "Now that Gina knows you're okay, I assume she'll tell your parents."

Emma groaned and leaned into him. He gladly accepted her weight, her burden, especially when she wove her fingers through his fur as she sought comfort.

Yeshe surprisingly liked this role, caring for someone, holding them in his arms. No one had ever consoled him, not even as a child, and he hadn't imagined he could actually comfort another person. He'd failed in providing the support Dorje needed last year, but thankfully, Gina came along and helped him through dark days.

"I have a surprise for you," he whispered as he held Emma.

Red-rimmed, watery eyes turned up to him. "Another one? I like your surprises."

"Sourdough chocolate chip cookies."

Her lips turned up into the smile he wanted to see. "Yum, Yeshe. How did you manage that without the stove—and without me seeing?"

He pulled her closer. "They're actually small pancakes, but my supply of chocolate chips is limited, so when I put them in pancakes, I consider them cookies and a special dessert. I made them while you were getting your canoe ready this morning."

A laugh burst out of Emma, and Yeshe's chest swelled. He wanted to see her happy, see her smiling and laughing. "Well, as we've established, I'm the twin that likes chocolate chips in her cookies." She both sniffed and giggled as she burrowed into him. Gods, he wanted more of this. He didn't want Emma to feel bad, but providing her comfort was, well, satisfying.

"And the sky is clear, so we'll have an excellent view of both the sunset and the sunrise."

Emma wiped at her eyes, then crooked her finger in a 'come here' signal. He bent down, and she placed a kiss on his cheek. "Thank you, Yeshe, for your support and kindness."

His face warmed. Turns out he loved receiving Emma's tender peck as much as her scorching, passionate kisses.

"I knew I'd have to tell my family the truth, but I didn't imagine it would interrupt my trip." She paused, then added, "Or interrupt my time with you."

Heat from his cheeks spread through his whole body, and he suddenly wanted more time with Emma. His long-buried fear of abandonment suddenly resurfaced. A panicky sensation flared in his chest, just as he'd experienced as a kid whenever his parents were about to leave again.

But Emma had to go. She had a life, and it wasn't here on Little Caribou Creek. And this was why Yeshe kept most people at a distance. He tried to bury these new feelings of attachment and attraction for Emma, even as he allowed himself to reach for her hand. She might be heading home soon, but he'd make the most of the time they had together. "Come on," he said, pulling her toward the camp stove. "Let's eat and get up to the lookout for sunset."

She squeezed his hand and offered a smile, despite her red nose and puffy eyes. "And sunrise," she added.

After they ate, Yeshe led Emma up the hill, winding through birch forest and highbush cranberry shrubs that would turn red and pungent in fall. He took her hand to help her up a steep section. She didn't let go once they reached even ground. Yeshe enjoyed his first hand-in-hand stroll through the woods.

"The overlook is right through these trees," Yeshe explained as they neared their destination.

As the view opened before them, Emma released his hand and scampered up a rocky outcrop, squinting as she looked out into the distance.

"Do you like the view?" Yeshe asked as he sat on a boulder.

Emma huffed a soft laugh. "I've been contemplating views. A bad view brought me to Alaska. As you know, I moved into the corner office at work last year," she explained as she settled herself in his lap. "I have floor to ceiling windows on two walls."

"Sounds nice and bright," he said. It seemed like it would be anyhow, especially farther south where winter days weren't as dark.

"Yeah, not so much. My long-awaited view includes other corner offices and two dark, narrow alleys with dumpsters."

Yeshe tried to picture city buildings, Emma's real life. It didn't appeal to him. He didn't want Emma anywhere but in Alaska, in his arms. He tightened his hold, hands sliding down her shoulders and arms, coming to rest on her thighs.

They were both silent for a moment, as they took in the low angled sun on the horizon. Its final rays cast a soft golden glow over a mosaic of green flatlands and sparkling waters in the distance.

"Every day in Alaska I've been blown away by the views." She rested against him and his chest vibrated with a contented purr.

"This isn't bad," he agreed, gesturing toward the setting sun. "But my cabin doesn't have a view."

Emma tilted her head and looked up at him. "I disagree. What about the creek, your cache, the green hills in the distance, and the big birch tree next to your shower? And," she added, "every morning when I opened my eyes I saw you. I liked that view the best."

At a moment that should have been calm, serene even, as they watched the sun dip below the horizon and pop back up a short while later, Yeshe's heart raced. Emma had officially wrecked him. He'd broken all his rules by developing feelings for her. How would he say goodbye to her in a few days without breaking his own heart?

CHAPTER FOURTEEN

Three days on the river sailed by as swiftly as a lost paddle in the rapids. For the third night in a row, Emma tossed and turned in the tent by herself. Tonight, regret and anxiety weighed her down. Tomorrow, she would need to face her family and say goodbye to Yeshe. Her heart squeezed at the thought of leaving him.

Finally, she gave up on the tent and dragged her sleeping bag out to Yeshe. She curled into his welcoming arms and threw the unzipped bag over herself to keep the mosquitos from eating her alive.

She woke up some time later to soft caresses along her back. When she let out a groggy hum of pleasure and snuggled deeper into her yeti, he slipped his hand beneath her shirt. Firm, large fingers kneaded sore paddling muscles and dragged a groan from deep within her.

"I like waking up this way," she mumbled against his soft fur. He chuckled, the gentle tremble of his laugh passing from his chest to the palms of her hands, which she'd pressed flat against him.

"With twigs and leaves in your hair?" he teased, his gravelly morning voice making her tingly with the need to be even closer to him.

Emma pushed the sleeping bag off her shoulders and realized it had only covered her face, and her hair was, in fact, a wild mess. She glanced up at Yeshe, his sapphire eyes warm and alive this morning. "I can't even imagine what I look like."

Yeshe's gaze flickered, like a flame going from low to high as that impossible blue darkened into the sexiest hue Emma had ever seen. She felt the vibrations of his growl before she heard it.

"Beautiful," he rumbled, his leg moving between hers. "Gorgeous." He shifted her back until she lay sprawled on her sleeping bag while he rolled over her, his forearms braced on either side of her body. He dipped his head, his lips so close to hers. "Tempting."

She took in the warm-blue of his sun-kissed skin, the snowy-white of his beard that bordered on untamed. The past week she'd loved the sensation of his fur against her cheeks, and the tickle as it slid down her chest and tantalizingly brushed against her thighs. She nearly whimpered, wishing all her clothes, and his, would simply melt away.

Emma blinked up at Yeshe. This was the view she desperately wanted again and again. This was the view that made her happy. This was the view she would never, ever forget.

Their clothes did disappear in a blur of urgent pulls and tugs. Desperate kisses shared between unzipping, yanking, and flying buttons.

When nothing separated their naked bodies but a warm morning breeze, Yeshe braced above her once more, hot, pulsing, and notched between her legs. They'd had sex standing up in his shower, him from behind, and her on top. They'd even done the deed on his kitchen table. But they'd never tried the missionary position. He braced himself on his elbows, the weight of him and all that glorious fur teasing her skin, making her body and soul come alive. It felt good, right, and she arched up, encouraging him to slide in, slide home.

"Emma," he growled, as he slowly pushed into her until their hips were flush and she was blissfully stretched and full.

"Yeshe," she gasped, her legs coming around him, skin sliding against fur, hard muscle flexing beneath her grip as he tipped his head and gave her the most thorough kiss of her life.

He eased out and inched his way in again, setting a slow, bone-melting rhythm.

This wasn't sex for sport or pleasure alone. Yeshe was making love to Emma. Her heart hammered as she gripped him tighter and kissed him with more passion than she realized she possessed.

What started slow quickly built. Emma met Yeshe's thrusts with her own fevered desire, needing everything he could give her. Sweat slicked her body as he stroked into her. Their moans, grunts, cries of pleasure, no doubt flushing birds from the trees. As Yeshe broke above her, his face straining with his release, Emma came too under his fierce gaze.

She whispered his name as she drew him closer still. He lowered himself against her, while holding the bulk of his weight in the most disciplined plank ever—giving her just enough, exactly what she needed without crushing her. "Thank you," she whispered in his ear.

He nuzzled her neck and kissed her shoulder. "It's me who should thank you. You're incredible, Emma." He lifted his head to regard her. "I'm glad your pilot had no sense of direction." He paused a beat. "You'll text me the moment you're back in Anchorage, won't you?"

Tears pricked the corners of her eyes as she nodded. "The very instant."

It overwhelmed her to consider how much she'd need to deal with once she returned to the real world. This trip had changed her, and she realized in that moment, lying beneath Yeshe, his length buried deep inside her, that she'd outgrown her old life. She couldn't return. She wasn't the same person. There was no going back.

The transformation had been happening slowly —maybe it'd begun with her first tattoo. But her time in Alaska had sealed the deal. Emma had changed and her life needed to as well.

Before the well-trained disciplined part of her could slam on the brakes and try to control what was in her heart, Emma blurted, "What if I stay? I want to stay with you, Yeshe."

He blinked down at her, panic written all over his face as his dick slid from her body. It seemed to retract fully into his sheath.

She'd scared him. "Yeshe, I—"

He rolled to her side and cut her off as he brushed a finger across her cheek, but his crystalline gaze didn't quite meet hers. "Little bird. I'm not going to be the one to clip your wings."

Emma pushed up on to her elbows. "You're not. If anything, meeting you has made me feel freer than ever. Being with you makes me happy, and I haven't been happy in a really long time. I want to stay in Alaska, and I want to be with you."

Yeshe chewed on his lip a moment, as if in thought, before he finally looked directly at her. "Emma. This was temporary. A fling. We both agreed to that."

If this was a fling, then why had he just made love to her more tenderly than any of her previous partners? She bit her cheek, willing her body to suck back the threatening tears. This was about Yeshe, not about her, not about them.

With all the strength she could muster, she said, "In Wildwood, you said that life was full of risks. This is one I'm willing to take. I'm going to quit my job and move to Alaska, Yeshe." Forcing a smile was harder than cutting a firebreak, but she managed something weak. "The view is incomparable," she said, gripping his hand. "I'll be waiting for you when you're ready."

YESHE'S HEART raced as he looked down at Emma. He wanted to believe her—not that he thought she was lying. They'd just made love, no two ways about that. He'd never done that before. No woman, no person meant as much to him as Emma did. But what would she think of the *view* once she'd returned to Anchorage, then her East Coast life? Their fairytale time on the river had ended. Forest princesses didn't exist, after all.

Yeshe's parents had claimed they'd cared for him, but in the end, he'd always been alone, neglected. No matter what Emma said right now, he knew better. She'd realize her mistake and change her mind as soon as she boarded her flight out of Alaska, if not sooner.

Emma's fingers laced with his, and she squeezed. "I'll be waiting for you," she repeated.

"Emma . . ."

She pressed a finger to his lips, stopping his protest. "It's okay, Yeshe. I'm not trying to talk you into anything. I only want you to know where I stand." She paused a moment, gaze sure and steady on his, anchoring him in place while his gut reaction told him to pull away and protect himself. He wanted to believe Emma, but the fear of giving in and being abandoned again made his belly ache.

Emma sat up and abruptly changed the subject. "I should find my buttons. This shirt won't close without them."

Yeshe, glad for the new topic, felt a hot blush sweep his cheeks. Right. He'd ripped her shirt open. "I can replace it," he said, as Emma plucked a button out of the sand next to the sleeping bag they'd just made love on.

"No need," she said, then exclaimed, "Oh, here are two more." She held her palm out to him with a grin, but the smile didn't meet her eyes. "Three's good. I have a sewing kit in one of my bags."

"Dorje may have thread and needles too," he offered. She sat there naked, a vision of beauty, with her fist closed around three buttons while her eyes looked suspiciously glassy. Guilt consumed Yeshe. But rejecting her now was better for them both. It was.

As he tried to convince himself of this, his nose twitched. Yeshe leapt to his feet as he sniffed the air.

"Smoke," Emma said from beside him. She'd stood as well. "I smell it too. You should check in with your fire crew."

He nodded while pulling out his phone and sat comm. Was she giving him permission to leave? To flee? But it wouldn't be fleeing if his crew needed him. He'd simply be doing his job. So why did it feel like a flimsy excuse after spending several days together?

A message from Nima waited for him.

Nima: Fire on Eagle Knob. A float plane can pick you up at your cabin. We'll create a firebreak for the village of Coho. The rest of Aurora Crew is on the way.

"They need me," he said, glancing from the message to Emma, who still cradled the three buttons in her hand like they were all she had left of the special moment they'd shared and their time together. Gods, he hated this. He never should have given in to his attraction. "I have to go," he said. Guilt gnawed at him. Not only did his actions and words hurt her, but he was also about to abandon her on the creek shore, miles from her charter pick up.

Emma nodded in understanding and then reassured him, as if she knew he needed it. "It's okay, Yeshe. I planned this as a solo trip. I'll be fine." She gently set the buttons on the tree stump next to her sleeping bag. "Unless you need my help packing your things, I'm going to clean myself up in the river before getting dressed."

Yeshe shook his head. Preparing to fight a wild-fire was easier than dealing with feelings. "I got this."

While Emma plunged nymph-like into the creek, Yeshe clumsily yanked on his pants. He gave himself a mental shake and refocused on the task at hand. Retrieve his firefighting gear. Meet Nima. Save a village from a destructive fire. He hastily broke down his raft and packed his belongings.

Emma swiftly bathed and dressed again. She wore her button-up shirt over a T-shirt, its sides flapping open in the breeze thanks to its missing buttons.

He searched her eyes. "You'll message me?"

A smile ghosted over her lips. "Every day."

That wasn't . . . He shook his head. "I meant, will you message me when you make it back to Anchorage?"

Her small smile didn't waver. "Yes," she said, "and every day after that."

His chest tightened at the promise, still sore from a childhood full of disappointment. She meant well, but Emma would forget him. One day, the messages would stop coming.

Despite this, he allowed himself one last indulgence. Yeshe scooped Emma into his arms. Her legs effortlessly encircled him as she twined her arms around his neck. He crushed his lips to hers, not wanting the fireworks to end. But they would. They'd fizzle like sparklers in the rain. As he finally lowered her back to the sand, he said, "I'm never going to forget you, Emma."

She gave him a matter of fact look. "Of course not. I won't let you. I'm staying in Alaska, Yeshe." She backed away, as if making it easier for him to leave. "And I'll message you every day."

He wanted so badly to believe her. Yeshe took one step back, then another. "Goodbye, Emma."

She gave him a sad but knowing smile. "Goodbye for now, Yeshe."

Yeshe turned and entered the woods, hastily making his way back to his cabin for his plane ride to Eagle Knob.

Just like that, Yeshe was alone. And once again, he had to convince himself that he was better off because of it.

CHAPTER FIFTEEN

Emma's trip on Little Caribou Creek ended like it started, paddling alone down a winding, idyllic stream. But heartache and nervousness replaced the excitement that had coursed through her a week ago. Thoughts of Yeshe filled her mind, except in those moments when the anxiety of facing her family took over. Then worry caused her stomach to ache and her hands shake.

Emma navigated the lake, arriving at her pick-up location. The charter plane arrived on time—and at the correct location. The pilot, a woman in her forties with silver streaks in her dark hair and laugh lines around her eyes, instilled confidence in Emma. She apologized for the drop-off mix-up on behalf of the company and assured Emma they would reimburse her for the flight cost. Within minutes, the plane buzzed along the lake and lifted into the sky.

Emma craned to look back at Little Caribou Creek far below, but the pilot pulled her attention in another direction. "That's the Eagle Knob Fire," the pilot said, voice crackling over Emma's headset as she gestured to a line of smoke in the distance.

Emma's gut clenched for an entirely new reason. Yeshe. He'd soon be out there, potentially risking his life. "I have a . . . friend who's been called to fight the fire."

"I worked on fires for three seasons when I was in my twenties," the pilot shared. "A tough job. I don't regret it, never made better friends, but I'd rather be flying above all that smoke than on the ground inhaling it."

As the fire shrunk to only a plume on the horizon behind them, Emma pictured Yeshe when he left camp that morning. He'd nimbly hopped over a downed tree as he'd begun his return trip to his cabin. She might be anxious about his safety, but Yeshe was fully capable and at home in the woods, on the ground . . . And she'd likely need to remind herself of this in the coming days.

The plane soon descended toward Lake Hood, and Emma spotted Gina and a giant, well-covered person by her side. At a moment when Emma should have been proud—she'd accomplished her goal, completed a week-long paddle trip in Alaska—her stomach sank. Not only had she basically offered her heart to Yeshe, and he'd rejected her, but now Gina *and* Dorje were about to scold her—and rightly so—for her irresponsible decisions.

But when Emma walked off the floatplane dock, a beaming Gina ran up and engulfed her in the biggest hug ever. Soon Dorje's arms came around them both. "We're so glad you're okay, Emma," he rumbled, locking them in an embrace so loving it brought tears to her tired eyes.

As they broke apart, Gina slung an arm around Emma and Dorje hefted her gear, canoe and all. "You," Gina said, squeezing her sister tight, "have been holding out on me. Dish. I want to hear everything."

Emma's anxiety eased, and her shoulders relaxed a fraction. This wasn't the reaction she'd predicted. She'd expected disappointment from Gina and Dorje because . . . well . . . The truth hit Emma in the gut. Because if the roles were reversed, if Gina had lied about an ex-boyfriend and a secret trip and worried their parents, Emma would have been disappointed in Gina. The truth stung as

Emma viewed herself and her sister in a new light. "I'm sorry. I shouldn't have lied about Derek or my trip."

Gina waved a dismissive hand. "Don't be sorry. I don't want to second guess your motivations, but believe me, I understand the urge to follow where your heart leads. And frankly, I'm just glad that your heart led you away from Derek. You are so much better than him."

"I agree, but then most people are," Emma said, huffing a dry laugh.

Dorje placed all her gear in the truck's covered bed, and they climbed in the front. As soon as Gina buckled herself in, she spun as far as her seatbelt allowed to face Emma.

"Okay, I want to hear it all. Derek. Your planned trip. And," Gina said, waggling her eyebrows, "I want to hear about your week with Yeshe."

A blush, hot and fierce, swept across Emma's cheeks. "First, I need to send him a quick message to tell him I made it back safely."

Gina squealed. "Didn't I tell you, Dorj? I knew they had chemistry."

Emma's face flamed as Dorje gave Gina a conspiratorial smile and stole a glance at Emma in the rearview mirror. She powered on her phone, ignoring the other text and email messages that awaited her.

> Emma: Made it back to Anchorage. Dorje and Gina picked me up and weren't horribly mad at me.

Picturing the smoky edge of the Eagle Knob Fire, she added another note.

> Emma: Stay safe.

Yeshe responded immediately, as if waiting for her message.

> Yeshe: At my cabin. Of course, they understood you needed the trip. Take care, little bird.

How had he covered so much ground so fast? Didn't matter. He'd made it home safely, even if his turnaround would be fast. Yeshe had understood and supported her trip all along, but his tolerant attitude struck her anew. Emma might not have been so sympathetic if roles were reversed. One more way she could change for the better.

Her thumbs hovered over the keypad before she tapped out one more message.

Emma: I miss you.

A moment later, a sharp sting on her palm made her realize she'd clenched her fist so tight while waiting for a return message, her fingernails had left crescents on her skin. She shook out her hand and tucked her phone in her bag. Yeshe missed her, she was sure, even if he didn't say it. She unzipped her jacket pocket and thrust in her hand, eager fingers quickly worrying her swallow charm.

"Start from the beginning and spare no detail," Gina begged, "especially when it comes to Yeshe."

Emma filled Gina in on her breakup with Derek, including the body art he never saw.

"Hold the phone, Holly Hobby," Gina exclaimed. "You have how many tattoos?"

Emma chuckled at her sister's reference to dolls they'd had in their youth. "Five now," she admitted. "But I only had three when I broke up with him."

"I'm abso-fucking-lutely in awe of you," Gina declared. "My twin sister has ink, rebellious ink." She glanced to Dorje and back. "I don't even have any body art. Why don't I? I might need some ink."

Gina copy Emma? That hadn't happened in years. Emma flipped her hair back and turned her head to show her sister her Gemini tattoo. "If you're interested we could get matching tats."

After a moment in which Gina did nothing but blink, she slowly lifted her hand and gave Emma the sign of the horns. "I'm one hundred percent on board with that idea." She turned to Dorje and said, "Babe, I'm going to get a tattoo to match my twin."

He squeezed her knee. "You have to do it."

"Right? I do, I totally do," she said before turning back to Emma. "Now, about your trip. How did you plan all this?"

"Agnes helped me," Emma admitted, hesitating, uncertain how Gina would react to her next confession. "She's my emergency contact, and I've been in touch with her daily."

"Aggie?" Gina cried. "Of course she helped you. Why didn't you guys tell me?"

Emma shrugged. "Because I thought you'd try to stop me or . . ." She swallowed. "Or join me. You're already known as the adventurous sister."

Gina cast a sidelong glance at Dorje, but didn't refute Emma's comments.

"Plus," Emma added, "Agnes and I weren't sure what you were up to since we hadn't seen pictures of Dorje. Of course I get it now, but Agnes is still in the dark about yeti."

"Who's Agnes?" Dorje asked.

"Emma's friend from college," Gina supplied. "She's an attorney who specializes in environmental law." Gina turned back to Emma and asked, "Did you tell her about meeting Yeshe on the creek?"

Emma shook her head. "You ask that like there's something to tell."

Gina gave her a wicked grin. "I know there's something to tell. But what's still a mystery is how you came to be on Little Caribou Creek. Was that your plan all along or did you change your itinerary once Yeshe taught you how to use *his* . . . er . . . *a* stick?" Her eyes were full of mirth at her double entendre, and she snickered into her hand.

"Ha. Ha." Emma didn't stop her eye roll. "Neither," she said. "The charter company screwed up and dropped me at the wrong location, and I didn't realize it until after the plane was long gone. I'd planned to float Birch Creek."

Gina gasped. "What? No. So you're in the middle of nowhere all by yourself and decide to float a new creek?"

"The guidebook said Little Caribou was navigable, and it also empties into Big Bear Lake, my pickup destination. I gave it a shot."

"That, dear sister, is truly badass." Gina had

never used that term to describe Emma. She liked it, especially coming from her twin. Gina continued, "And then you floated right past Yeshe's cabin?"

Her skin warmed at the intimate and thrilling memories she wasn't about to share—Yeshe rescuing her from a fire, their wild outdoor shower sex, and him thoroughly searching her body for hidden tattoos. She managed a casual shrug. "Yeah, sorta. We ran into each other."

Gina made air quotes as she repeated, "'Ran into each other.' I know what that means." She smirked. "Okay, sis, what next? Where's Yeshe?"

"Headed to the Eagle Knob Fire," Emma shared, her shoulders bunching once again.

Gina turned to Dorje. "Is that the new fire you mentioned?"

"Yeah, started by lightning midweek," he responded, glancing at Emma in the rearview mirror. "Our friend Nima, also a yeti, is working this fire, too. They'll both be fine," he assured Emma, as if he sensed her tension rise with the topic.

"Thanks," she said. "I'm sure you're right. Yeshe's been fighting fires for years. As for what's next . . ." She paused and blew out a long breath before sharing her big news. "I'm quitting my job and moving to Alaska."

Gina blinked. "No fucking way." She blinked again. "You're serious?" When Emma nodded, Gina squealed and covered her face with her hands. "Oh my god, this is so exciting!" She turned to Dorje. "Let's take her by Mari's grandparent's house tomorrow." Gina spun around. "It's a super cute place that's for sale by owner. Are you still flying back to Philly the day after tomorrow?"

Emma confirmed with a nod. She was moving to Alaska, but she still needed to quit her job, pack her apartment, and break the news of her move to poor Agnes, who was ready to leave the East Coast herself.

"The house has a detached building, Em, perfect for a certain yeti who might want to set up a wood-working shop here in town."

Her heart sped at that news. Despite Yeshe's claims that what they shared was temporary, Emma liked the idea of having a home Yeshe could easily move into. "I'd love to see it," she admitted, "but Yeshe . . . well, he may not be interested in an in-town woodworking shop." She didn't add "or me" but based on the knowing looks that Gina and Dorje gave each other, she didn't have to.

"He's scared of close relationships," Gina added.

Emma had gathered as much. "Terrified. He's

been disappointed in the past. But I never back down from a challenge. I won't let him down."

Twisting farther in her seat, Gina offered her sister a high five. They smacked hands as Dorje said, "You're exactly who my brother needs."

Emma's middle fluttered. She wanted to be the person Yeshe needed. Because he'd become someone she needed. "Also, before I leave, I'd like to visit some local stores to gauge their interest in carrying Yeshe's hand-carved items."

Gina bounced in her seat. "That's a great idea. His wooden ornaments would be a hit at the new boutique in Wildwood."

Emma thought back to Yeshe's sourdough pancakes. "Perhaps Wildwood Bakery would sell their dry mixes in Yeshe's bowls with a carved spoon as a gift set."

Gina flapped her hands in excitement. "I would totally buy that!" Emma loved seeing her sister's enthusiasm on Yeshe's behalf.

When Gina calmed, she gripped the seat again and took a deep breath. "Dorje and I have discussed it, and we're going to tell Mom and Dad about yeti. No more secrets in this family. We'll schedule a video chat with them when you're ready. You have big news—what with your job and, well, everything."

Emma nodded, thankful for her sister's understanding. "I also owe them an apology."

"No rush," Gina assured her. She turned to face forward, then squealed again. "My sister's moving to Alaska!"

Dorje chuckled and squeezed Gina's knee. "We'll need to set up weekly dinners. Don't extended families do that?"

"Oh," Gina said excitedly, "Yeshe would love-hate that!"

Emma agreed, and her heart clenched. The idea of attending family dinners with Yeshe at her side and potentially sharing a house, no, a *home* with him, excited her. Of course, she first had to convince him to take a chance on her.

She had a lot of ground to cover over the next few weeks—quit one job and apply for a another, pack an apartment, and find a new home in Alaska. And through all this, Emma aimed to ease Yeshe's fears and win his heart.

YESHE WRANGLED the last chunk of spruce tree root out of the ground and tossed it aside. Upslope from him, Nima's chainsaw roared to life as he sliced through a downed birch. After several long days of hard labor by themselves, the two yeti had managed a significant firebreak through the forested hills outside the town of Coho.

Yesterday, they'd been shrouded in smoke. Today, it drifted to the east, leaving them views of the valley they hoped to protect. They had more work to do, but their efforts had gone a long way toward helping spare the small town from the advancing fire.

When the chainsaw's buzz fell silent, Yeshe strode over to Nima. "Time for a break?" he asked before heaving a freshly cut log out of the way.

Nima palmed a large branch in his leather-gloved hand and grinned. "You just want to check your messages."

An image of Emma—mahogany hair, moss-green eyes, and knowing smile—filled Yeshe's mind. He fought a frown as he gripped his tool handle so tightly the wood threatened to splinter. She'd messaged him every day, as promised. But he couldn't message back. He wouldn't lead her on. She *thought* she'd continue to message him, but she wouldn't. People said a lot of things they believed in the moment. It didn't mean they would follow through.

Emma had returned to Philadelphia. Would she think about him today? Remember to send a message? Yeah, he was certain she would. But what about tomorrow? Or the day after that? She *said* she wanted to move to Alaska, but would her feelings change after sleeping in her own bed for several days, after the novelty of her trip wore off? Packing her home and moving thousands of miles seemed daunting to Yeshe. Truthfully, it would be much easier for her to stay in Philadelphia.

"I always check my messages when out on a fire," Yeshe said matter-of-factly.

Nima cracked a branch in two over his knee and tossed it aside. "True, but your brother's messages don't soften your eyes or make you smile like you're about to pet a kitten. You must be getting texts from Emma." At Yeshe's frown, Nima raised his hands as if in defense. "I'm not judging. I'm glad you have someone to look forward to after you're off the fire."

"You're reading this all wrong." Yeshe tapped his Nomex clad chest. "Remember, I'm the established bachelor, the loner who lives in a little cabin in Middle-of-Nowhere, Alaska. I'm not looking forward to anyone, and if someone is looking forward to me, they're in for disappointment."

The laugh lines around Nima's eyes faded. "I

see," he said. He braced a boot on the downed tree and scanned the view. In the distance, wisps of smoke curled over blackened forest where the fire had already burned. Just before Yeshe looked away, Nima said, "I know what it's like to be in love, too."

Yeshe blinked. In love? He snorted as he lowered himself onto a large rock and pulled his satellite communicator and phone from his backpack to power them on. No reason to waste precious batteries when the closest electrical outlet was a helicopter ride away.

"I'm not in love," Yeshe asserted. "I've only known Emma a short time. Not long enough to fall in love, of all things. Plus, I'm not the falling in love type." Yeshe was certain that making love differed from being in love. Almost one-hundred percent certain. Yes, he felt affection for Emma, but how could it be love?

"I've only been in love once," Nima admitted, "and you probably don't want advice from me, but it seems like love doesn't follow any rules. Doesn't matter if it's days or years."

Yeshe huffed. "You're right about the advice part. This from the guy who broke poor Mari's heart."

Nima's features sobered. "I've made a lot of

mistakes. I don't deny it. If I can spare someone else the same pain I've felt, it's worth making a furry ass out of myself."

"If you don't mind making an ass out of yourself, apologize to Mari." Yeshe couldn't believe he was having this conversation. Nima and Mari separated years ago, and in all that time, he and Yeshe had never once talked about their failed relationship or Yeshe's lack of a personal life.

Nima's white eyebrows creased, and he looked genuinely remorseful. "If only we'd straightened things out early on. Too much time has passed for that. I'd be opening old wounds. Besides, Tseten says Mari's well. Wildwood Bakery recently hired her as head baker."

Yeshe didn't miss the pride in Nima's voice, and he carefully crafted his next words. "It's never too late to say you're sorry, Nima." If only he'd heard those words in his youth. If only his parents had made some small acknowledgement of the pain they'd caused him, maybe it would have made a difference. Their indifference had only added to his pain.

"Would it help her or ease my conscience?" Nima's next words were barely audible. "I don't want to hurt her again." He fell silent as his chest rose and fell. "I don't know what happened in your past, Yeshe. But don't let those experiences ruin what you have now. Don't let an opportunity to love and be loved pass you by. It doesn't get better with time if you don't deal with it now."

Yeshe took a deep breath as Nima's advice washed over him. Clearly, they both had past trauma they needed to work through. Nima meant well, but he was misguided. "I appreciate your advice, but it doesn't apply here. Emma is a friend, nothing more." The words felt oddly bitter on his tongue, but he spoke the truth, didn't he?

Nima shrugged in response, then stood straight and dusted off his gloves. "I'm starving," he declared, changing the subject. "Do you have any sourdough pancakes squirreled away in your pack?"

Yeshe pulled a face. "If I did, they'd be moldy by now. Gotta make do with another MRE."

Nima perched on a rock near Yeshe and opened his pack. "Right. Well, Chicken Burrito Bowl it is."

"Better than Chicken Chunks," Yeshe commented as he turned his attention to his phone. Emma might only be a friend, and he might not have any intention of writing her back, but Yeshe couldn't wait another moment to read her latest message.

His app showed three new texts . . . all from

Emma. His mouth went dry. Was this the day she'd explain she wasn't coming back to Alaska after all? And why would he care? If she returned, they'd simply be distant friends, one-time lovers. Nothing more. The same as if she chose to stay in the Lower Forty-Eight.

He tapped the screen to open her chat and immediately relaxed his shoulders. She'd sent messages and *pictures*. She wouldn't send selfies in her last-ever text, would she?

> Emma: Philly is hot and humid, and my hair is big and frizzy. Check out *my* creek!

Yeshe studied Emma in the accompanying photo. She wore a raspberry-colored tank top, thin straps over her smooth, strong shoulders. A shadowy hint of cleavage graced her neckline, and he immediately pictured the swooping curve of her perfect breast. His heart and his groin clenched. Gods, what this woman did to him. He finally looked past Emma and the auburn-tinged ringlets framing her face, to the lush green forest behind her and the ribbon of water through the trees, fascinated at this glimpse she'd shared of her world.

He saved the picture to his phone—as any friend might do—then scrolled to her next message.

> Emma: Delivered my resignation letter and cleaned out my office! *raising hands emoji*

Yeshe paused, then reread the message. She'd actually resigned. Left her job. His throat convulsed in a nervous swallow. Would she move to Alaska after all? And was it because of him? He'd only disappoint her—he hadn't even responded to her messages. Why did she keep thinking of him? What did she expect from him?

With sweaty palms and a racing heart, he scrolled to the next message and second picture.

> Emma: Me and Agnes packing up my apartment. Alaska or bust!

Another selfie. Once he dragged his gaze from Emma, he saw a dark-haired woman taping up a box, an empty room in the background. This was real. Emma intended to move to Alaska. But what did it mean for him?

Yeshe glanced at the final message.

> Emma: I miss you *heart emoji*

His heart clenched so tight he thought he might keel over. He missed her too, so much. But he had to push those feelings away, bury them deep. He lived alone by choice for good reason. It might hurt now, but they'd both get over each other.

A gust of wind and whiff of smoke pulled Yeshe out of his own head. Nima, bag of dinner in one hand, spoon in the other, paused to look out over the valley. "Weather's changing," he observed as the breeze ruffled his fur, and the acrid stink of wildfire smoke grew stronger.

Yeshe quickly powered down his devices, glad for the distraction. He needed to eat, and they needed to keep moving. He didn't have time to moon over Emma. He shouldn't be thinking about her anyway. The time they'd shared on the creek had been the best of his life, but temporary and fleeting, by design. A little pain now would save them both from much bigger disappointment and heartache in the future. Life experience had taught him this was true, but as he quickly prepared his meal, he couldn't stop thinking about Emma.

Agnes slouched in one of the two folding camp chairs in Emma's otherwise empty living room and propped her feet on a moving box. "Emma, you've been my best friend since college. I don't understand what's happening here . . . You go on a one-week trip, meet a guy, don't snap a single picture of this great new mystery man—or Gina's boyfriend —and now, you're moving to Alaska. Two weeks ago, I would have described you as steady and stable, and voted you least likely to up and move to a frozen land of penguins."

Emma held up her hand. "Penguins don't inhabit the northern hemisphere," she corrected.

Agnes blinked at her. "That's all you have to say? You didn't even take a picture of Gina's new boyfriend." She narrowed her eyes. "I'm beginning to think these two brothers are vampires or something, that their pictures can't physically be taken."

Emma forced a laugh. If only Agnes knew how close she was to the truth. "They're very sensitive, that's all."

One could most definitely take Yeshe's picture. Emma had a few in a locked folder on her phone, including one she'd received yesterday from Tseten, of all people, with a heart-fluttering anecdote. Nima had inadvertently captured Yeshe in the corner of a photo he'd sent to Tseten. When he'd asked about Yeshe's moony expression, Nima had responded with a laughing emoji and an explanation that the photo had caught Yeshe reading one of Emma's much-anticipated messages on his phone.

Sure, she loved knowing Yeshe enjoyed her messages, but it left her confused. If he appreciated her texts, why had he only replied once? She hadn't heard from him since the day they parted. She'd blamed his silence on his firefighting duties, but learning he'd chosen not to respond, well, it hurt.

She wouldn't let it discourage her, however. Especially not after seeing him so captivated by her message. Emma had promised she'd wait for him. And she meant to keep that promise. She hoped he would eventually trust her as completely as she'd trusted him to carry her from danger when trapped by the fire.

"Well," Agnes continued. "It seems like you and Gina have met nice people in Alaska. Some computer programmer—Tseten? I think that's his name—followed me on LinkNet. Said he was Gina's friend and had recently met you."

Emma couldn't stop a choked laugh. "Tseten friended you?"

Dark eyebrows creased Agnes's forehead. "Why is that funny? I checked him out. He has a lot of professional followers on the site and he follows you, too."

An image of Tseten, a giant, furry, gregarious yeti walking around Dorje and Gina's potluck shaking everyone's hand came to her mind. If only Agnes could really know him. "It's not funny. He's great, super nice guy and a respected professional, I understand."

Agnes crossed her arms. "I feel like you're not telling me something."

Ugh, this was hard. Emma now understood how challenging it had been for Gina to keep Dorje a secret. "There's nothing to tell," she began, her face heating, when her phone alarm pinged, saving her from telling more lies. "Oh, sorry Aggie, I have a call with my family in fifteen minutes." Her stomach pitched with nerves. "I'll be apologizing to my parents for lying about Derek and my trip." Even mentioning it to Agnes dried her mouth.

Her friend's face pinched as she swung her feet to the ground and stood up. "Yikes, sorry, Em. I'll get going." She came over and gave Emma a hug. "I guess you'll also be breaking the news about your resignation and move."

Emma let out a shaky breath and nodded. "Yep," she said. "All the fun stuff." During the call, Gina planned to reveal Dorje to their parents, too. Emma intended to tell them about Yeshe as well, but, of course, she couldn't tell Agnes about any of that.

As soon as Agnes left, Emma closed her eyes and took several long, slow breaths, attempting to calm her nerves. Then she positioned her phone on a stack of moving boxes and adjusted a camp chair in front of it. Her phone rang with a video call as she settled herself with a glass of water by her side.

Gina appeared on the screen, and Emma assumed Dorje sat right out of view.

Their parents connected, but their video showed a ceiling. "Is this on?" their mother asked. "Can you hear us?"

"We can hear you," Emma and Gina both confirmed.

Their mother's shoulder appeared, then the ceiling again, before her face came into view. She smiled into the screen. "There are my beautiful girls," she said, adjusting her camera until both their parents came into view. They all said hello, then their mother gushed, "Oh, Emma, we are so glad you're okay."

A knot formed in Emma's gut. "I'm really sorry for worrying you." She took a quick sip of water to combat her nervous, dry mouth. She needed to explain her motivations and intentions quickly. Rip off the bandage.

"I shouldn't have lied," she began. "But for a long time now I haven't been happy."

Her mother let out a small squeak, nothing judgmental, more of a, "I don't want my daughters to be unhappy" type sound that squeezed Emma's heart. Their father wrapped his arm around their mother, and Emma pushed on.

"I've been successful at school and work, and I'm proud of that, but I may not have been setting and pursuing goals for the right reasons," she paused. "I wasn't happy at work or with Derek. When we booked—or when I thought Derek had booked—the float trip and we enrolled in canoe lessons, I finally had something I was excited about."

"Derek never booked the trip," Gina quickly added in an exasperated tone before waving a hand. "Sorry, your story, Em. I'm still steamed up about it. I'd like to mail him a raw salmon via ground shipping. Know how long that would take? Weeks. I'd love to see his face when he catches a whiff of that."

While Gina cackled, Emma couldn't help a snort of laughter. That *would* be funny. She shook her head to clear her thoughts and continued, "Gina's right, he didn't book the trip. By the time I found out, it was full. So, I—"

"Dumped his sorry ass?" Gina blurted again, this time raising a hand in a virtual high five.

"Sweetie," their mother interjected. "Let Emma finish."

Emma appreciated Gina's solidarity. "Yeah, I dumped his sorry ass. I packed up his stuff and left it in one of his mostly empty penthouses." After a pause, she added. "I hadn't thought to leave a dead fish."

Gina beamed. "There's still time."

"Ladies. Enough with the dead fish," their mother pleaded with a scowl before returning to

Emma's story. "So, then you planned your own Alaskan trip?" she asked.

With a shrug Emma said, "I did. And I was afraid if you all realized my intention to go alone, you'd try to stop me. But I had to do this. Had to prove something to myself."

"I took a solo hiking trip once," their mother said as she glanced at their father.

Emma and Gina shared a surprised look before Gina asked, "You did? When was this, Mom?"

"Right after college. But I got turned around on the trail and met, er, another traveler. We hiked together after that." She cleared her throat. "It was a life-changing experience for me, so Emma, I can't judge, and I wouldn't begrudge you your experiences. But please be assured that we will be there to support you."

Their dad added, "Of course we support you. And for the record, I support the fish plan." He gave their mother an apologetic side-eye.

Emma huffed a laugh. "Thanks, Dad. And thank you, Mom. That means a lot, especially as I have more news." Her parents both straightened, and though it was off-camera, she could have sworn her father took hold of her mother's hand. "You may have noticed that my apartment walls are bare. I've submitted my resignation, and I'm moving to Alaska."

"She's going to be my neighbor," Gina squealed. "She's already made an offer on a house down the road from me and Dorje."

Their mother steepled her hands over her mouth as if overcome by emotion. "My girls are going to live near each other?"

Their dad hugged her close. "You don't know how happy that will make her," he said of their mom. "And me too, of course."

"Oh," their mother cried. "I can't wait to visit and finally meet Dorje." She paused, hesitating before asking, "Is he home today, Gina?"

Gina's face grew serious, and Emma's middle squirmed with nerves. She really hoped Gina's news went over well. After all, Emma was also in love with a yeti.

Her breath caught. In love with Yeshe? Gina said something into the camera, but Emma didn't catch it over the percussion of her beating heart. She loved Yeshe, she realized. He might not be responding to her messages, but she was even more determined not to give up on him. On them.

Then Dorje appeared on the screen next to

Gina. "Mom and Dad," her sister said, "I'd like you to meet my boyfriend, Dorje."

Emma watched the two video feeds on her phone screen. Gina rested a hand on Dorje's broad chest. They both looked nervous, worried. Her parents, on the other hand, both blinked, mouths slack as Dorje greeted them. "Hello, Gwen, Tom," he said, his white, furry arm wrapping around Gina. "It's a pleasure to meet you at last."

Their father pointed at their screen. "Is he," he began, turning to their mother as if for confirmation before correcting himself. "Are you—"

"A yeti," Dorje supplied. "I'm a yeti."

Their father turned back to their mother. "Your hiking friend was—"

Her cheeks flushed with a rosy blush. "A sasquatch," she squeaked.

Emma sucked in a breath as their mother's confession sunk in. Meanwhile Gina cried, "Wait, what?"

Their father cleared his throat. "Your mother met a sasquatch on her solo hiking trip," he supplied. And although it hardly seemed possible, their mother turned a deeper shade of red. "So, we knew more beings exist than most people realize." He gave a friendly wave to the camera. "It's very nice to meet you, Dorje," he said. "Gina has told us all about you . . . I think. You *are* a mountaineering guide?"

Dorje confirmed as much, and the conversation went back and forth in a warm, but slightly awkward, "new boyfriend meeting the parents" kind of way until Gina interjected, making a time-out signal with her hands.

"Can we rewind?" She asked, "*Sasquatch* are real?"

"They're real," Dorje confirmed.

Gina gaped at him, probably much like Emma gaped at her phone. "We are chatting later, mister," Gina playfully warned Dorje.

But Emma still focused on the coincidence. "Mom, *you* met a sasquatch while on your hiking trip?"

"Dated," their mother corrected as she tucked a strand of hair behind her ear.

Emma let out a chuckle as Gina squealed, "No. Way."

While her mind was still whirling at this news, Emma had more to tell her parents. "I met someone while in Alaska," she shared. "His name is Yeshe, he's Dorje's half-brother, and he's also a yeti."

Their mother laughed. "Where is Yeshe?" she

asked, while their father added, "We'd like to meet him too."

Emma bit her cheek, then explained, "I like Yeshe. A lot. But Yeshe is . . . Well, he's not on board —yet."

"Are you returning to Alaska to woo your yeti?" their mother asked, beaming.

A prick of happy tears stung the corner of Emma's eyes. "I'm moving to Alaska for me, but I fully intend on wooing Yeshe," she admitted, loving that she had the support of her family.

As they chatted about future visits to Alaska and offers to help her move, which she politely declined, Emma felt a sense of calm settle over her, similar to how she'd felt when she'd been with Yeshe.

Her unhappiness with her job, her ex, and then lying about her trip had weighed heavily on her. That weight had lifted, disappeared. And she'd finally come to accept both herself and Gina for who they were, not who Emma thought they should be. Gina and Emma were more alike than Emma had ever realized, and for once, that pleased her.

Emma's future filled her with excitement. She would focus on her happiness first, for once, not on what she believed others expected of her. And she aimed to convince a big, wild, firefighting yeti to take a chance on love. On her.

YESHE JERKED AWAKE. The sweet, dreamy vision of Emma writhing beneath him in his bed quickly faded as a dull backache reminded him he currently dozed on the hard, uneven ground. For several weeks, he'd drifted off every night after reading Emma's most recent message. And every night, she'd graced his dreams.

Emma was stubborn and relentless. He hadn't returned a single text since she'd safely returned to Anchorage. He'd done nothing to encourage her. Yet, every day, she sent him thoughtful messages about her return trip to Pennsylvania, job resignation, move to Alaska, and house purchase. Emma and Dorje were close neighbors now.

She'd done everything she'd promised. And every single text to Yeshe included an unwritten message: "I'm thinking about you. I haven't forgotten you. You are important to me." It all stirred emotions in Yeshe that he couldn't identify and left him confused and uneasy.

Yeshe rubbed sleep from his eyes. Not far from

him, Nima sat up as well, and they both turned to a large aspen a few yards away swaying in a stiff breeze. Clouds lined the horizon, though not a drop of rain fell. With the overcast sky, Yeshe had to check his watch for the time: four a.m.

"Is the wind coming from the north?" Yeshe asked as he massaged a sore shoulder.

Nima, face smudged with dirt, stiffly rose to his feet. "Yep. That's not a good direction for us. We need to monitor that ridge."

"No doubt," Yeshe agreed.

The radio squelched with static as Nima picked it up. "I'm calling in."

As he touched base with the rest of their crew, Yeshe turned to scan the ridge above them. A single plume of dark smoke suddenly shot skyward—likely a dead tree had ignited just over the top. It was close. Too close, especially with this wind.

A pulse of adrenaline shot through Yeshe, and he hoisted his pack as he called out to Nima, "We've got activity above us."

Nima gave him a silent nod of acknowledgement while the radio buzzed with static and garbled information. "The fire's changed direction. It's coming toward us."

That much seemed clear. "It's time to make for

the safety zone. Let's retreat to the saddle," Yeshe said. "We'll cross the stream and make our way down the valley to the spike camp." Stream was a generous description for the trickle of water that descended the mountainside. Despite its size, it could be a natural firebreak. Unless the wind picked up even more. Then the fire could jump the creek.

Nima took one last glance at the ridgeline as he tightened the straps of his pack. "Good call. Let's go."

They wasted no time leaving their temporary overnight camp, which flames could soon overrun. The area lacked appreciable undergrowth, and Yeshe and Nima made good time as they descended a gentle slope through the forest. The footing was sure, but the air quality deteriorated. Smoke wafted over the ridge behind them while also rolling in from the front, intensifying as they neared the stream. It became so dense that Yeshe hadn't realized they'd made it to their destination until he'd splashed into the narrow waterway. "This doesn't bode well."

They'd only made it several hundred yards downstream when a sudden, scorching gust of wind slammed into them, carrying the acrid bite of smoke and stinging black ash. The dull roar of an inferno grew ahead. "It's no good," he called to Nima.

Nima, mouth to the radio again, motioned for Yeshe to retreat. "Back up the hill," he called.

Normally, this type of situation would have triggered a primal survival instinct in Yeshe. He wasn't an adrenaline junky, but most yeti were in tune with the natural world around them, like many wild animals. And a wild animal in its prime rarely became a victim to wildfire.

Instead of instinctually knowing what to do, where to go to save himself, a surge of panic gripped his chest as thoughts of Emma filled Yeshe's head. He'd never written her back. What if something happened to him and he never could? What if she never knew how much her messages meant to him? She thought of him every day. No one else ever had. Why had he pulled away from her when she decided to stay? Why had he mistrusted her and his own feelings?

Yeshe stumbled, didn't see the rock until he pitched forward. A large hand shot out and caught him.

"Easy," Nima cautioned.

Yeshe ran a trembling hand down his face. "I don't know what's wrong with me."

His friend smirked. "You're in love, Yeshe. You're in love and in danger, which means your thoughts are squarely on Emma when they should be on saving your own ass." With a grimace, he added, "Ask me how I know. I might have broken up with Mari years ago, but it doesn't mean I stopped loving her." He slapped Yeshe on the back. "Come on. Our only option is up this slope. Let's hope it isn't burning on the other side, because you have dozens of text messages to respond to."

On top of the adrenaline that coursed through Yeshe, a stab of embarrassment jabbed at him as he quickly strode alongside Nima. "How do you know I haven't responded to Emma?"

Nima huffed a laugh. "Tseten, who else? You're not writing her back, but he's asking me about you so he can fill her in."

Yeshe could only shake his head. He should have been updating Emma directly. He'd never been the subject of Tseten's gossip—that he knew of, anyway. And it wouldn't be the last. When he made it out of this inferno, his first stop would be Emma's new home in Wildwood. News of his epic grovel would spread through the yeti gossip channels faster than this wildfire, but Yeshe didn't much care. Not if Emma forgave him.

Yeshe reached the top of the rocky slope a few steps ahead of Nima. His stomach sank at the view before him. Fire converged from both the north and south, leaving a narrow strip of unburned forest ahead of them. Beyond that, his gaze lit on their possible salvation. "An airstrip," he called back to Nima. No vegetation to burn, just a thousand feet of gravel. He mumbled a thanks to the patron saint of small aircraft pilots for their past construction efforts.

"A fucking gauntlet," Nima observed as he paused beside Yeshe. "These trees are all dead, killed by spruce bark beetles."

"A tinderbox." As soon as the words left Yeshe's mouth, an old spruce tree exploded into flame, lighting up like New Year's Eve, sparks showering into the unburned area. *Fuck! I have to get to Emma!* The thought of not touching her, holding her in his arms, or apologizing made him nauseous. It also solidified his resolve. "We're going to thread this fucking needle." He grabbed a handful of Nima's shirt. "Come on. It's shrinking as we speak."

Both yeti tore down the hillside as more trees flared around them. Dead pine needles littered the ground and hid loose rocks. Yeshe's boot hit one, and he windmilled his arms as he lost his balance and went crashing to the ground, smashing onto his shoulder. He slid down the steep slope on his side, reaching for tree trunks to slow his momentum, but he couldn't gain purchase. His fingers scraped against rough bark. He finally wedged his boot against a downed tree, jerking to a stop and pain shot up his leg. He wanted to shake his head, clear the daze, but the other end of the downed tree burst into flame.

Emma. Yeshe had to get down this hill in one piece so he could see her again. A sense of clarity shot through him, and he pushed to his feet. As he did, Nima let out a yell. Yeshe quickly glanced back, only to find his friend also sliding down the steep slope. Yeshe lunged, grabbing Nima's outstretched palm, stopping him seconds before he crashed into the tangle of burning branches. "Gotcha!"

"Shit," Nima grunted, toes too close to the flames. He kicked his booted heels into the dirt, scrambling backward as Yeshe used all his strength to haul him away from the burning tree. Once clear, they both scrambled away from the fire, half running, half sliding out of the zone of dead spruce and into green birch trees less prone to flaring up like gasoline poured on a bonfire.

"Anything broken?" Yeshe yelled to Nima, wincing as he stumbled forward on a throbbing ankle.

"If it is," Nima said, face pinched as if in pain. "I'll find out once we're down this hill."

"Too true." Yeshe swallowed a grunt of discomfort as his injured shoulder brushed a tree trunk as he rushed by. "We're almost there."

The slope soon leveled out, and they reached flat ground before stumbling from the forest onto the edge of the airstrip. Both yeti half jogged, half hobbled to the center of the inflammable gravel. Yeshe fell to his knees once they'd cleared the danger of burning alive and stopped to look back at the slope they'd tumbled down.

What he saw made his stomach queasy. Flames fully engulfed the hillside. Yeshe ran a trembling hand down his face. "That was close."

"Too close," Nima agreed, swaying on his feet. He caught himself, then gave Yeshe's hand a firm shake. "You saved me from becoming a roasted yeti marshmallow."

Had he though? Yeshe took in the tear in Nima's shirt sleeve and darkened sooty fur. "Nima, you're bloody and your fur is singed."

Nima glanced down to the spot on his arm that Yeshe indicated and frowned. "Looks no worse than your shoulder."

Yeshe followed his friend's line of sight to a large

tear in his own shirt. His arm didn't hurt until he saw the blood. "Fuck," he murmured.

Nima raised his radio to his face. "Fuck is right," he said. "Time for the team to get us the fuck outta here." He grinned, teeth gleaming-white against all the ash and soot darkening his fur. "You have a lot of messages to respond to and someone waiting for you back in Wildwood."

An unfamiliar sense of hope washed over Yeshe as he pictured Emma, and he smiled back at his friend. "I do. And I'm going to do everything I can to make it up to her."

CHAPTER SEVENTEEN

When Yeshe realized his knuckles had turned a light-blue, he made himself unclench the armrest of Mari's truck as she drove him to Emma's new house. Several weeks ago, it had been Emma who sat in the passenger seat, fists balled, on their drive into Wildwood.

"You sure you don't want to shower first?" Mari asked, glancing at him, then back to the road.

Yeshe dipped his head toward his armpit but only caught a whiff of smoke. "Do I smell that bad?" After the helicopter had rescued him and Nima, he'd taken a quick dip in the creek at the spike camp and changed his clothes. He looked forward to an actual shower, but he had other priorities. "I want to see

Emma first," he said. He needed to explain himself and apologize.

"Only a little eau de forest fire smoke and a spicy 'I haven't properly showered in weeks' perfume," Mari said with a chuckle. "Don't worry, Emma won't care. But . . . why didn't you call her for a ride? She knows you're coming, right?"

His grip tightened on the armrest again. "Um, no. I'm surprising her."

Mari side-eyed him. "Right. So, you're showing up at her door after not responding to any of her texts—"

Yeshe nearly choked as he cut Mari off. "Is everyone aware that I didn't respond to her texts?"

"Mostly, yes. But don't worry, we all understand. I don't even think you'll have to do any groveling, Yesh," she admitted, before quickly adding, "but you should."

"I'm prepared to grovel," he said, wincing when she gave him a reassuring pat on his sore shoulder.

"Are you hurt?"

He rotated his arm, as if that would ease the ache. "Nima and I had a close call yesterday, but we'll heal." He recalled Nima's declaration of love for Mari. Did she still care for him, too? "Nima is also okay," Yeshe added as casually as he could, gauging her reaction from the corner of his eye.

Mari adjusted the chain around her neck and let out an exasperated sigh. "Tseten already filled me in, though I don't know why either of you bother to keep me up to date. Nima's an ex. I haven't talked to him in years. Save it for his current girlfriend."

Yeshe almost opened his mouth to correct Mari, tell her Nima wasn't seeing anyone. But he thought better of it, reflecting instead on his own situation. If this was how it turned out when couples hurt each other's feelings but didn't talk or apologize, Yeshe wanted no part in it. He already knew how bad that could be between parent and child.

Although nervous as hell, Yeshe sighed in relief when Mari turned into Emma's dirt, tree-lined driveway a moment later.

"If this doesn't go well," Mari said as she slowed in front of the house that used to belong to her grandparents, "I'm right next door." Despite being Emma's nearest neighbor, the wooded property and rolling terrain hid the other house from view.

Mari smiled as if to put him at ease while she pulled out her phone. "I don't think you're going to need me, but I'm texting Emma that I dropped someone off at her door. It wouldn't do to scare the crap out of her, surprise or not."

Yeshe climbed out of the truck and grabbed his bag. "Thanks, Mari. I owe you one."

She winked and gave him a knowing smile, then called out the open truck window, "Have me over for sourdough pancakes when you get settled in with Emma."

Yeshe's mouth opened and closed. Settled in with Emma? He wanted to apologize and make things right with her. He hadn't considered what would come next. He turned to the familiar two-story log home. Dorje's grandmother and Mari's grandparents had been friends, and Yeshe had regularly visited years ago. But now, he saw the snug house with its wide porch and back deck in a new light. He saw possibilities, potential, and a future with Emma. If she'd still have him. He hoped she would.

"I promise," he said before Mari waved goodbye and drove away.

Yeshe ascended the front steps, boards squeaking beneath him. He'd fix that for Emma. As he approached the front door, he saw her through the window. His breath caught at the sight of her, even more beautiful than he remembered. She studied her phone while descending the stairs from the second floor, mahogany hair swinging in a ponytail. But as Emma raised her head and caught sight of Yeshe, she stopped abruptly.

For a moment, he could only hear the hammering of his heart and blood surging through his veins as she stared at him. Though his mouth had gone dry, and a nervous tremor ran through his body, he tentatively raised a hand in greeting.

When a smile broke out across Emma's face and she ran to the door, a torrent of relief rushed through him. He still had a chance.

The door swung open, and there stood Emma, beaming up at him in a sleeveless shirt and short, summery skirt. His gaze traced the familiar curves of the honed muscles she was so rightfully proud of. "Yeshe."

His name across her lips sounded like a sweet melody from a summer songbird, and he couldn't help a hint of a smile. But a full grin wouldn't come until she accepted his apology. "Emma," he said in return. "It's really good to see you."

"I'm so happy you're here," she began before frowning as she regarded him. "But are you alright? I heard you and Nima had a narrow escape yesterday. I was worried about you."

He'd never had a closer call, but now that he was back with Emma, all seemed right in the world again. "We were in a tight spot," he admitted. "But we made it out with only a few bruises."

"Good, I'm so glad," she said, glancing at her phone, then back at Yeshe. "Mari dropped you off?"

He swallowed hard. Should he have asked Emma for a ride instead? It hadn't seemed right to ask her for a favor before apologizing in person. "She did . . . I wasn't sure . . ." How should he explain himself to her?

Gentle fingers brushed his forearm, sending a pleasant tingle up his arm. "It's okay, Yeshe."

"It's not," he insisted. "I owe you an apology, Emma. I'm sorry I pushed you away."

Her hand moved down his forearm, and she entwined her fingers with his, even now giving him silent support. A lump formed in his throat and his voice cracked as he continued, "I was scared. I spent my entire childhood with parents who disappointed me, pawning me off on others or leaving me by myself for extended periods. They were both yeti and semi-nomadic. They hadn't wanted a child. Each time they left, they were gone for longer than planned—months sometimes. And when they returned, they'd promise to never do it again, but then they would. I'd be alone again. Forgotten."

Emma's hand tightened on his. "Yeshe, I'm so sorry."

He gave a jerky nod. "I became distrustful. I never wanted to experience those emotions again. I avoided it by keeping people at a distance. By limiting my friends and staying out of romantic relationships, I never put myself in a position where someone could disappoint me. Was it lonely? Yes. But I'd spent my childhood alone—not by choice. At least as an adult, the choice was mine. I made a conscious decision to be the hermit yeti in a remote cabin on Little Caribou Creek."

"I understand," Emma began, her small thumb brushing over his knuckles. "Your childhood sounds terrible. I can't even imagine such a betrayal from your own parents. I'm so glad you had Dorje and his grandmother." She looked away, and a single tear rolled down her cheek. "I like you, Yeshe. A lot. And I respect the lifestyle that you've chosen for yourself. I didn't mean to pressure you with all the texts I sent, I—"

Yeshe sucked in a breath as a sense of panic raced up his spine. Did she think he was letting her down again? He cut her off as he dropped to his knees in front of her. "You didn't pressure me, Emma," he insisted, cupping her chin and swiping at a second tear with his thumb. "I want to be here with you. I'm simply explaining how and why I've lived a solitary life . . . until this point. But as you reminded me, life is full of risks. I don't want my old life. I don't want to look back on our time together and wonder 'what-if?'"

He brushed a strand of hair away from her face. "On the Eagle Knob Fire I lived for your texts. Ask Tseten or Nima. I read them over and over, then dreamed about you each night without fail. Initially, I didn't respond because I didn't want to lead you on. I figured you'd lose interest, especially when you returned home. But you didn't." He cradled her cheek with his palm. "And that confused me. I was scared. And each of your messages was like a kiss on the forehead, a reminder that you cared for me. I'm truly sorry I didn't do the same for you."

She shook her head. Her eyelashes were damp from her tears, but she smiled at him. "You didn't need to." She let out a small huff of laughter. "I didn't mean to spy on you, but Tseten took it upon himself to provide me with regular updates. Although I was unsure about your feelings toward my messages, I knew you were reading them, seemed to be pleased, and that you were well. I didn't need anything else." She glanced away, her smile widening. "Except you, of course. But I'm patient, and you're worth the wait."

Yeshe's heart clenched. People had shown him affection in the past, like Dorje and his grandmother, but this was different. Emma wasn't a relative or someone who had a maternal instinct toward him. She saw him as a partner, a lover, and she showed this affection because she cared for him. "Emma . . ." He croaked, his own eyes welling with unshed tears, his throat tight with emotion.

He pulled her toward him, sliding his arms around this incredible woman as he drew her flush against his chest. She twined her arms around his neck, hands gliding under the collar of his shirt in the most intimate way as her fingers wove through his fur. A low, satisfied growl rumbled from his chest.

"You don't have to wait any longer. I want to be with you, by your side. You're the only person I've ever cared about this way, and I'm ready to be vulnerable. Yesterday, when I thought I might not get this chance to tell you how I feel . . ." His heart raced with a refreshed sense of panic at the memory, and he pulled back slightly to look Emma in the eye.

Her lovely gaze didn't waver from his as he

continued, "I've never been in this type of relation-ship. I might make mistakes, but I'm going to trust my gut. Not taking a chance would be worse. True suffering would be wondering 'what-if.' I want to be with you."

He sucked in a deep breath and went for it. "I love you, Emma," he said, pausing as her eyes widened and her perfect lips parted slightly. "Will you accept my apology? I promise to make it up to you and do better next time."

Yeshe swallowed hard. He'd put it all out on the line. Emma knew how he felt and what he wanted. He expected the flight instinct to hit him, the urge to retreat to his cabin, to not get so close. But it didn't come. And now he could only wait for Emma's reaction.

EMMA HAD MADE SO many changes in her life over the last month, and they'd all felt right. She'd waited for her more practical side, the side of her that cared how others perceived her decisions to weigh her down, stop her momentum. But it hadn't happened. And now? The rugged, vulnerable, furred yeti on his knees before her, who'd grown to be the most important person in her life, had declared his love for her.

Yeshe *loved* her. And he'd been brave enough to tell her.

She couldn't stop her tears, even as she memorized her current view. Blurry, but the best yet. Emma had never thought about fate before this moment. Fate hadn't helped her through school exams or fast-tracked her promotions. She'd achieved success through hard work. Likewise, pure determination had brought her to Alaska. But everything about Yeshe had been out of her control or by chance —being at her sister's and Dorje's at the same time, the accidental drop-off on his creek, the fire and his rescue. She hadn't originally come to Alaska with a plan to change her life and fall in love, but that's exactly what had happened.

Emma laced her fingers behind Yeshe's neck. For the first time in her life, she readied herself to utter the three little words she'd never said to anyone outside her immediate family—not even her ex, which was telling. "I love you too, Yeshe." Her bottom lip trembled with emotion and anticipation of what their mutual declaration meant. "Thank you for trusting me with your vulnerabilities. I won't take it for granted. Also, don't worry about mistakes.

While I've strived in the past not to make them, I look back and see all my bad calls . . . like staying in a job and relationship that didn't make me happy. We're going to make mistakes," she said, palming the back of his neck. The earnest way he regarded her, with trust and affection, made her heart so freaking full. She couldn't get enough of this man. "We'll work through them together."

He gave her a slow, solid nod. "Together," he repeated, as if they'd made a sacred vow, which they very nearly had. Emma was overjoyed and bursting with happiness.

"We have a lot to discuss," she went on. She needed to share her plans and understand where he stood. He might love her but not be comfortable leaving his cabin. She really hoped he'd be open to more. "I've applied for a job with the Wildwood school district," she began. "If I receive a position, I'll need to be in Wildwood during the school calendar year. But in summer—"

Yeshe cut her off, nodding in understanding as he said, "You'll get to spend your time anywhere you want to explore."

She grinned but had to point out the obvious. "I realize it overlaps with the fire season, but I want to explore with you, when you're free. I want long days on the creek and longer nights in your bed as your forest princess."

Yeshe's eyes flared and the accompanying growl that vibrated his chest made Emma's cheeks flush with heat and longing. "I want that too, and not only during summer at my cabin." He slid a possessive hand down her back to cup her ass. "I want to warm your bed all year long. And if you're here for winter, then I will be too." He glanced past her to the house. "That is what you had in mind, isn't it?" He bit his lip. "I should confess, at least three people already messaged to tell me I could convert the old outbuilding into a wood shop."

Emma laughed. Despite not hearing a peep from Yeshe for a month and limiting her texts so as not to overwhelm him, their friends had done a lot of communicating for them. "Yes," she confirmed. "I hope it works for you."

He ran his other hand down her spine to rest against her lower back. "I'll love it."

"I'm glad to hear it, because I have other news to share." She rocked on her feet in her excitement for Yeshe. "Wildwood Bakery would love to collaborate with you and sell gift sets with their mixes, and your bowls and spoons. Both the bakery and Wildwood Cycles would like to carry the sets."

Yeshe blinked. "Both stores are on board?"

"Yep," she said with a nod. "You can negotiate this, of course, but they'll pay you sixty percent of the retail price." It pleased her to see Yeshe's eyes widen at the generous percentage. "I've also reached out to three other places, and all are interested in hand-carved items and will pay fifty percent of your set price."

"I'd have an income from my carving," he said, his tone suggesting he didn't quite believe it could be true.

"You're incredibly talented. And I'm hoping you'd like to use that talent to remodel some of the house—the bathrooms especially." She briefly closed her eyes, hands moving as she described her vision. "Hand-carved cabinets with a creek theme . . . I'm thinking fish, pebbles, and birds—swallows, of course. Then a heated tile floor leading to a large walk-in shower with two showerheads."

His eyes flashed again. "For us to shower together," he rumbled, his voice low and tone suggestive. Yeshe's fingers flexed against her as he glanced to the house and back to her. "What about today?"

He didn't wait for a response before he scooped her into his arms. Emma yelped in pleased surprise as he rose to his feet, cradling her against his body, one wide palm under her skirt, supporting her ass. As she wound her arms around him, he warned, "Mind my left shoulder. I banged it up yesterday." Emma took in a spot on his upper arm where his short sleeve rode up. His fur looked shorter, darker. Burned? "Oh my god, did you singe your fur?"

He grimaced. "Nima looks worse."

She kissed her fingertips and lightly placed them on his arm. "Does this mean I get to play nurse for you later? We have two small bathrooms to, erm, break in, if you know what I mean."

He pulled her tighter against him. "Oh, I know what you mean. Challenge accepted, little bird. And yes, I'll play patient to your nurse any day."

She released a deep, contented sigh as Yeshe carried her into the house—no, *their home*. Heat pooled low in Emma's belly while her heart leapt with blissful joy. Her promising future with Yeshe made her the happiest person ever.

AS YESHE CROSSED the threshold of the Wildwood house, where he planned to live with Emma, a sense of rightness washed over him. He didn't want to be alone any longer. The isolated protection of his cabin on Little Caribou Creek no longer appealed. He looked forward to him and Emma sharing dinners with Dorje and Gina, and hosting Mari for breakfast. But mostly, he looked forward to every moment with Emma.

"Little bird," he rumbled as he tightened his grip on her, fingers slipping beneath the band of her panties as he toed off his boots inside the front door. "If you have any plans today, you'd better cancel them now."

She laughed, her torturous lips nipping at his earlobe. "Why is that, Yeshe? Are you thinking we're going to be busy?"

If he had his way, they'd be *busy* for days. "I believe I have some groveling to do," he said, as he glanced up, recalling the layout of the house. He strode through the bathroom door and placed Emma on the counter, loving that her legs instinctively spread, making room for him to step between them.

"You don't need to grovel," she said, her fingers already working the top buttons of his shirt.

Yeshe flipped her short skirt up, exposing her enticing pink panties and silky thighs, twitching under his touch. He hooked an arm under her knee, then leaned down to press a kiss to her inner thigh. "I *want* to grovel. I'm in love with you, little bird, my forest princess, and I want to make you moan in pleasure until you're limp and sated." He spread her legs wider as he moved closer to her dampening center, the heady scent of her arousal making him drop hard and fast. "And then," he said on his own groan of pleasure, "I'm going to start all over again. Because it's not only today that we have each other, it's forever."

Yeshe had never imagined himself living in a house in Wildwood, with the woman he loved at his side and a kitchen table full of friends and family. Yet here he was, pushing aside empty dessert plates, before sliding a rough sketch to Emma for her first non-hidden tattoo. He thought she'd like his drawing, but his pulse spiked, nerves getting the better of him as he shared it with the love of his life—and everyone else who looked on.

"Yeshe," Emma gushed as she took in the image of a creek, intricate swirls flowing over smooth rock. "I love it." Her small hand found his knee under the table, her reassuring squeeze immediately soothing his pulse. She turned to the others and explained, "I'd like it to start at my shoulder and flow down my arm to my elbow, if the tattoo artist is able." She glanced at Mari, who only shrugged.

Mari had recommended an artist she'd previously used. But she'd been vague about her own ink, which none of them had even known about until recently. "My tattoo is small," she said. "You'll have to ask her what she can do."

"Beautiful work, Yesh," Gina said, as she leaned over Emma's shoulder to study his sketch. "After I get my little Gemini twinsies tattoo, I should commission my own piece from you. Maybe you and Dorje should get some ink too," she teased.

Yeshe huffed a laugh, the others at the table joining in. All except Mari, who said, "They'd have to shave first and then their fur would cover the ink once it grew back . . ." She trailed off, her cheeks turning a deep, cranberry-red. "Oh. You were joking." With all eyes on her, Mari let out an exasperated sigh. "Yes, Nima and I got tattoos years ago. We were young. And lucky for him, he has fur and can hide my name. I'm not so lucky. And no, I haven't had it removed, nor am I going to show it to you."

The group went silent for a moment as they exchanged glances, no doubt all thinking of Nima's newest construction job at a site near Wildwood. As far as Yeshe knew, Mari wasn't aware of her ex's upcoming plans.

Tseten slid a friendly arm around her, and she leaned into his side. In the doting big-brother voice that he sometimes adopted, he said, "Mari, did you know that Nima is going to be in town this fall? He has a house remodeling job on the outskirts of Wildwood, for a Creer and Associates attorney."

Mari's spine stiffened and the color drained from her face. She produced a wooden shrug, her facial features going neutral as she sat upright again. "Why would I care?"

Tseten blinked but quickly recovered himself. "Right, right. You wouldn't obviously, but I thought you should know if you didn't already."

Emma gave Mari a sympathetic smile. "Exes are hard," she said. "If it weren't for mine, we might not be sitting here discussing tattoos." When Mari looked at her blankly, Emma explained. "I basically covered my body with hidden ink in the hopes my ex would finally see me. He didn't."

Yeshe wrapped a possessive arm around Emma, and she leaned into him. "She's better off," he rumbled.

His comment broke the tension, and Mari

managed a weak grin. "Clearly. I'm happy for you both."

Happiness for Yeshe used to be a quiet day alone, ice fishing on the creek by his cabin. He'd never known true happiness until now. It nearly overwhelmed him as he studied Emma, who'd turned back to the tattoo sketch, her fingers tracing the headwaters of the creek.

Emma froze, her lips parting slightly. "This isn't just a creek. This is a woman's hair."

It wasn't a question. She turned to him, eyes wide and . . . Filling with tears? Yeshe's pulse spiked. "Is that okay? I can change—"

"No, no changes," Emma said, cutting him off as she snatched up the sketch. "Anyone want more coffee to wash down the second half of Mari's delicious pie?" she asked no one in particular. Then to Yeshe she said, "Come help me with the coffee," before she hastily stood and marched into the kitchen.

Yeshe ignored the murmurs around the table as he blindly scooped up two empty mugs and followed Emma. She stood in front of the half-full coffeepot, staring at his sketch while he set the cups on the counter.

Emma whirled to face him as she gestured to the

drawing. "These aren't just mountains," she said, her voice cracking. "It's a crown on a woman's head." Her lips silently formed the words, "Forest princess."

She'd seen it. He'd hoped she would but thought she'd have a different reaction. Yeshe rushed to explain himself, "I would have pointed out all the hidden symbolism before you had it permanently inked. But if you don't like it—"

Emma's palm landed on Yeshe's chest as she cut him off. "I love it," she said, tears now streaming down her face. She cinched her arms around him more tightly than anyone had ever hugged him. "I love it," she repeated, voice smothered as she buried her face in his chest.

His heart swelled as he gently untangled her from his middle so he could lift her into his arms. "I'm so glad," he confessed as sweet relief flooded his body.

Her arms and legs came around him while her tear-dampened cheek pressed against his. "I can't believe how much you packed into this heartfelt drawing, Yeshe," she whispered, her lips near his ear as she held up the sketch. "The creek with all its beauty and power. Me as the creek and . . ." She paused to pull back and smile. "Your forest princess.

Thank you so much. I am truly the luckiest person ever."

Yeshe smoothed a tear from Emma's cheek with the pad of his finger. "I think *I'm* the luckiest person ever."

"You're both freaking lucky," Gina said from the doorway. "This has been a lovely family dinner night but perhaps we should see ourselves out so you can . . . er . . . get even luckier tonight?" Her shoulders shook as she laughed at her own joke.

Before responding to her sister, Emma nipped at Yeshe's earlobe and in a low, husky voice meant for his ears alone said, "You *will* get lucky tonight, lover." As a shiver of anticipation ran through Yeshe, Emma addressed Gina. "We'll join you in a minute, but could you please grab the coffeepot and offer refills to the others?"

Gina lifted the pot and snagged Dorje's empty mug off the counter. "More pie for us if you stay in here. Just saying."

Emma rubbed her nose against Yeshe's. "We should join our guests, or they won't let us host again," she joked. "Plus, I want to plan your and Dorje's tattoos."

Yeshe's mouth quirked into a smile. "I would love your name written across my heart . . . Though it already is, whether permanently inked or not." It was the truth.

Emma tipped her forehead against his. "I love you, Yeshe."

He placed a slow kiss on her lips. "I love you too, Emma."

I hope you enjoyed Rescued by Her Yeti!
Please consider leaving a review.

Read about Yeshe's first anniversary gift for Emma in a free bonus scene!
www.nevapostauthor.com/rbhy-bonus

Learn how Mari and Nima really broke up. Can they make amends and live happily ever after? Find out in Married to Her Yeti

MARRIED TO HER YETI

A runaway yeti groom who stole her heart.

Mari's secret, estranged husband, Nima, may have ruined her for all other men, but at least her career is finally taking off. As she works with a lawyer to purchase her dream bakery, she also draws up divorce papers—it's time for a fresh start. But when Mari becomes injured, there's only one person in town over the holidays to care for her—Nima. He abandoned her after their wedding, so why is he sticking around now?

A love of a lifetime he can't let go.

After years of avoiding his hometown, Nima finds himself at the doorstep of the woman who shattered his big yeti heart. Mari crushes any hope of reconciliation when she hands him divorce papers. Wait—they're married? Stunned, Nima barely has time to process the revelation before an injury forces Mari to rely on him. She needs his help now, and he won't let her down again.

Caring for Mari is the second chance Nima never expected. But as she plans her fresh start, can he prove he belongs in her future—not just her past?

Alaska Yeti Series:

Ready for Her Yeti

Fake Dating Her Yeti

Yeti for Love

Rescued by Her Yeti

~ Coming soon ~

Married to Her Yeti

Loved by Her Yeti

Alaska Yeti Series Extras:

Catching Her Yeti

I'd be lost without my critique group! Heather and Elizabeth, thank you for your thoughtful insight, your wealth of grammar knowledge, and most of all, your support and friendship. And yes, I realize "be lost" is passive. I'm keeping it. ;)

A huge thank you to Jena for plotting with me WHILE hiking. The best combo ever! Your beta read and shared knowledge on watercraft and the firefighting world was invaluable. Dear reader, while I've tried to follow Jena's advice, and now know that an oar is not a paddle, but any mistakes in the book are mine alone.

I was incredibly lucky to receive thoughtful and positive beta read feedback from Aiden of Gleeful Gobin Reviews! Thank you for your time, insightful comments, and upbeat attitude. If I ever want to feel good about myself as I writer, I'll just go peek at your comments.

And once again, Kristin, my heartfelt thank you for your beta read and helpful comments and enthusiasm. I appreciate that you tried to slip in some extra sexy times, lol. Thank you for your tireless support!

Scott, I couldn't do it without you. Thank you for being my biggest fan and for proofing my books even if it takes extra strong coffee to get through them. Love you.

Dear reader, thank you for making it this far. I can't tell you how much every social media like, sale, and page read means to me. I appreciate you!

ABOUT THE AUTHOR

Neva Post grew up in a log house in Interior Alaska where she walked uphill both ways to school at temperatures of negative forty with only the aurora borealis to light her way. At least, that's how she remembers it.

She's equally happy on a snowy trail or coaxing vegetables to grow in her garden during the long Alaskan summer days. When she's not waxing skis or chasing voles out of her cabbage, she's at her computer. Neva's novels include paranormal elements—she can't help it—with smart and dependable characters who always get their HEA.

www.nevapostauthor.com

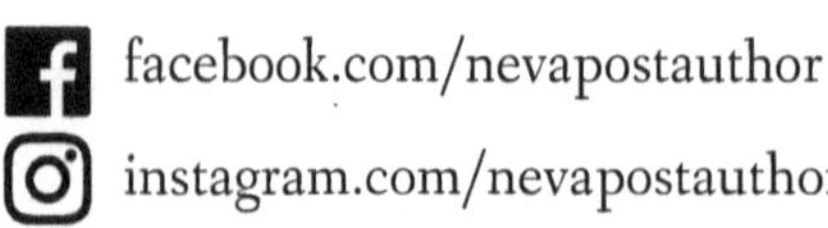

facebook.com/nevapostauthor

instagram.com/nevapostauthor

9 781958 830086